Carnivores

J. Cortex

Published by Lantern House Publishing, Nanaimo, B.C.

https://www.lanternhousepublishing.com

Edited by Nicholas Wilson.

Cover Design: Barandash Karandaschich/Shutterstock.com

ISBN: 978-1-9991734-2-5

Don't miss the next novel from J. Cortex:

Witch Bones

More from Lantern House:

Sugar Skin
Trial 23
Blackwood Manor
Witch Bones

Lantern House Publishing

Table of Contents

Carnivores

HORACE, THE TIME KEEPER

**Violence begets
violence**

J. Cortex

1

A dozen vehicles were ahead of Horace when he
pulled into the narrow lane of the Canadian-American
border crossing, just south of Vancouver, British
Colombia. He was surprised by the amount of traffic.
It was a chilly Tuesday in the middle of May, one week
before the long weekend. Why were so many of his
fellow Canadians making the journey South? He
supposed anyone's vacation could start at any time, and
America was an easy route of escape, just an hour
from the city.

Horace understood the country's allure, too.
The land of the free. The wild west. The lights of
America's bustling cities and the empty darkness of her
expansive countryside; the thick drawl of the southern
hicks and the whole nation's violent history, the
endless possibilities. Perhaps most enticing was the
heat. Even in May Vancouver was hard pressed to
push above 20 degrees Celsius (68F). For anyone who
lived outside of B.C, the idea of warmth was ludicrous.

Horace had crossed the invisible barrier
between frozen North and bountiful South twice
before in his life. The first was in his youth, in the
seventies. It was a different place then, but still
wonderful to explore. Horace had gone in search of
the party, of course. As a young man he wanted to
discover the beautiful women of California and capture
one or two, maybe three. He yearned to see the
splendor of the Grand Canyon, the salt plains of Death

Valley. He wanted to drink himself stupid in New Orleans, gamble in Vegas, and buy a few cheap whores in Reno. And he did. Horace and his best friend blazed a trail across the western states and enjoyed the temptations that single young men with a motor and two hard dicks between them tend to enjoy.

Horace figured not much had changed in the last forty years regarding that, and he assumed at least one of the cars in line was packed full of party seekers intent on winning a fortune in a noisy casino and participating in enough five-minute sex to last a lifetime. His money was on the two behind him in the beat up 1992 Buick Century, their wrap around shades and backwards hats emblematic of such pursuits.

Horace's second trip (twenty years after the first) had been of a lighter tone, and was driven by substantially less devious motives. It was a family vacation, likely what most folk crossing the border were about to embark upon.

Horace, his wife, and his two teenage daughters climbed into the family station wagon and took to the interstate. They were in pursuit of adventure, kooky road-side attractions, natural wonders, and Mickey's palace of tall rides and over-priced hats. They, along with hordes of tourists, flocked to Zion National Park for two nights of overcrowded camping and mobbed hiking trails. They gawked at the glorious chasm in Arizona alongside hundreds of others. They even went on a fully booked tour of Alcatraz.

It was three weeks of hotels, sing-alongs, parks, thrill-rides, star gazing, and bonding.

He had taken all three of his girls to America in the early nineties, before cell phones occupied the hands, minds, and eyes of not only young people, but all people. It was a time when a ride in the car was just that: a ride in the car. No screens for distraction. No social media for communication. Those stuck in Horace's white station wagon learned and played games, enjoyed the sights, read books, and talked. When camping, there were no electronic comforts. They roasted wieners and played cards, told stories and fell asleep to the sounds of nature.

Horace had a feeling those humble indulgences were no longer the key to a satisfying family road trip.

Horace Steeple glared at the few cars left ahead of him, and those in the returning lanes, and felt pity for vacations bedeviled by complaints of poor Wi-Fi and bad reception. He felt nostalgia for the simple days of friendly neighbours, and a great animosity for the new era of greed, paranoia, and terror. Horace caught a glimpse of two young boys seated in the back of their parent's SUV, each youngster's face bleak and zombified in the glow of some handheld device, the world around them falser than the one in their grip. He hated social media for making everyone feel so goddamn special.

He missed the years before the link, before the connection of everything and everyone. Furthermore, he missed his family. Horace smiled at the recollection of that trip long past, at the image of his smiling, dark haired brats, and his young, vibrant wife. It was one of his fondest memories, and two others sprang to mind after it.

The first was his and Susan's Greek honeymoon. They spent two weeks sipping wine in fancy restaurants and having newlywed sex on luxurious mattresses. Sunset cruises and couple's massages, old temples made for dismissed gods. The hot sun and the warm Aegean Sea. It was the most explosive time of his life, when the whole world appeared bright and hopeful, his goddess beside him. It was at some point during the honeymoon that Horace planted the seed for his eldest daughter, Lilly.

His second most memorable, and perhaps proudest moment occurred in his fighting prime. It was the day Horace beat the smug look off Winter's face in the second round. The cocky black bastard had egged him on for months until the two men, both in their strongest years, met in the ring.

Horace had been known at the time as 'The Knockout Clock.' 'The Time Keeper.'

One, because he knocked anyone and everyone out cold. Two, because everyone knew it. They knew from the moment the bell rang it was only a matter of time before Horace Steeple's fists shut off his opponent's lights.

That's exactly how it had gone with George Winters. An initial round that was more akin to a ritual dance than a fight started them off, and a second round, more akin to a street brawl than a boxing match, finished the day. Horace flattened Winters and beat his black face even blacker, sending him to meet the mat unconscious. No one ever saw George Winters after that, and Horace Steeple never displayed another whirlwind performance in the ring again. He won every fight after until he retired at thirty-two, but never with as much flare or passion.

That glory was gone now. Horace Steeple's time in the limelight had faded along with his eyesight, red gloves replaced by dorky spectacles. His juvenile vision of an infinite world had vanished as the years crept by, and a responsible, moderate opinion of tomorrow rose in its place, with the future of his daughters and his own retirement taking precedent above all else. His lavish taste for living dried up, molted, and became as blotchy as his flesh. His temperament turned senile long before he would get a chance, and once his youngest kid left home and five years later Susan died, Horace's forecast for the rest of his life grew quite grim.

In honesty, for the last half decade he had continued to work in the same factory that he had been employed at since he quit boxing, waiting for the day he would die.

2

On this May afternoon, Horace Steeple was sixty-three. He was a parent of two, a grandparent of three, and a widower. Lilly, his oldest, had married well. Gloria had *done* well. They were as secure as could be, and required no assistance from their ornery old dad, who still, to spit in the face of age, remained a bull.

Horace, although done with life, refused to stop exercising. He was as strong at sixty-three as he was at fifty. He never smoked and rarely drank. Horace knew that if his spirit willed it, he could have another ten or fifteen years of health and sound mind, but it was not until he was at the gates of America that he desired to keep those years.

Whether it was the adrenaline, the nerves, the intense pounding in his heart not felt in an eon—or the blood still oozing out of his knuckles, fusing his leather gloves to his busted hands, he did not know. It might have been the thrill of fleeing Canada as a murderer, the sly concealment of his raw fists below the gloves, his blood-stained t-shirt beneath a wool sweater he had handy in his truck. It also could have been the rush from the scene to the border, knowing full well he would be fingered and locked up if he did not escape right away.

Really, it was the sum of every feeling

associated with the slaying of those three men that made Horace want his life back. Watching the crimson mixture of their blood and his blood and the water from the gas station faucet spiral down the drain—seeing his face splattered with human essence—made him hunger for resurrection.

And he could have it. Only two more cars to freedom.

3

One car left.

Horace watched the driver of a beat-up Pontiac argue with the border guard. When the Pontiac pulled away, it turned recklessly down the U-turn ramp back to Canada, and the officer in his wraparound shades was left with a scowl on his fat American face.

The light went green and Horace pulled the truck forward. He stopped in the designated spot and let the camera snap his picture, laughing internally at the thought of his photo already posted next to the guard's monitor. *WANTED: DEAD OR ALIVE* scrawled across it, then proceeded to the booth.

This was it. If somehow Horace's identity had been discovered and cycled through the system, he would leave in handcuffs and spend the rest of his miserable life behind bars. Two hours ago, he would not have cared. Now he did. His body trembled as the officer laid that stern, indifferent policeman gaze on him and said, "Passport."

"Right here."
The guard took Horace's passport to his computer and scanned it. "What's the purpose of your visit to The United States of America?" he asked, using all the fervor of a loyal patriot.

"Retired."
Horace never thought it possible to be as nervous as he was then. In his old age, things like

anxiety simply ceased to exist. Now it held him in its unholy grasp. Luckily, he was indeed old, and if Horace appeared a bit shaky, he doubted the young cop would notice.

"I suppose it's my last chance to see America the ol' fashion way, four wheels and gasoline. Kids are all gone, eh, the wife too."

The gatekeeper stared at his screen, unimpressed by the same story told a thousand times. "Horace Steeple, when was the last time you entered The United States?"

"Oh, must have been twenty years ago now, maybe more. Took the wife and kids back then, eh. They're all gone now. It's just me."

After a long period of staring at the screen and chewing on air, the overweight sentinel turned to Horace, holding firm to his passport. "How long do you plan to stay in The United States?"

Yes! The man was clueless. He had no idea Horace was a killer on the run. A wave of relief washed over Horace as he said, "Three weeks, maybe four."

The patrolman craned his head to look beyond Horace and into the back cab. It would have been hard to hide anything back there. A quick scan showed nothing but receipts, coffee cups, and some clothing.

"One month it is, Mr. Steeple." He handed back Horace's passport. "Drive on through and enjoy your visit."

"Thank you, officer. I will."

The red and white portcullis lifted and Horace drove down the lane, past the *back to Canada* off ramp, and was soon on the highway, the feeling of freedom and adventure so synonymous with America trickling into his soul.

4

Horace drove non-stop to Bellingham, about twenty-five miles south of the border. He spotted a sign offering up McDonalds and a few other dining options, and took the exit. He parked in front of the restaurant's doors, turned off the ignition and went inside. He needed food, a drink, some napkins, and a moment to think.

Normally, Horace Steeple would never have ventured beneath the golden arches; but hey, he was a man on the run. His spirit was free. He gazed at the menu and let three customers go ahead before he figured out what to order.

A beautiful young girl, who he thought was Hispanic, greeted him. "Welcome to McDonalds, what can I get for you?" So devoid of enthusiasm that Horace had to smile.

"I'll take a big-mac and fries, please, and a coke to drink. Thanks."

"That it?" she asked, looking, but not really looking at him.

"Yes. Thank you."

The washroom was public but had no lock, and so he was unable to take off his gloves and check his open wounds, lest a stranger stumble upon the bloody mess. He settled for a quick inspection of his face and found it clear of blood. The stains on his undershirt were not yet seeping through the grey wool of his sweater, and so he left the washroom satisfied.

Horace returned to the dining area, retrieved his tray of food and sat in the corner. It was time to think.

The RCMP (Royal Canadian Mounted Police) had not wired his name over the border yet, but they would. He killed three men with his bare hands in front of an audience, in a very public place. Horace

Steeple would be on the evening news. That meant he needed to be far away and under a rock. No credit cards. No calls to his kids. No hotels that required I.D. He would also need to ditch his truck, or at least the plates, and find some new clothes.

Cunning and ambition flowed into the old timer in a way he had not experienced since his forties. He requested a pen and a chunk of paper from the Hispanic girl and made a list.

1. Money
2. Clothing
3. Vehicle
4. Sleep

Seemed simple enough.

Horace finished his coffee and greasy food, which made him feel ill, jammed his list into his pocket and politely discarded his trash in the bin, then retreated to his truck with a head full of ideas.

5

Money was easy. Horace had kept a perfect line of credit since his twenties. He had four credit cards with four different banks, a savings account, and a chequing account, not to mention his **RRSP**, which would now be impossible to access. That one stung. The pool he had filled his entire life was now off limits, and he would never get to swim in its golden waters. Ironic, he supposed, that when he finally wanted to retire the funds were locked up.

At least the credit cards were easy. It would take weeks for the police and the credit bureau to close him out. Across from McDonalds he found an ATM and pulled the maximum withdrawal amount from all four cards and both his bank accounts.

Carnivores

Horace walked back to his truck with close to ten-thousand dollars in American currency. The thought of being mugged never occurred to him. He simply strolled across the parking lot with the stack of twenties nearly spilling out of his hands.

Being the time savvy fellow Horace happened to be, he decided to scratch off most of his list while still in Bellingham. He found a Walmart on the outskirts of town and gathered up a few pairs of jeans, two knit sweaters, a jacket, a pack of socks, underpants, and a bundle of long sleeve shirts. He also filled his cart with oatmeal, fruit bars, nuts, vitamins, a flat of water, rubbing alcohol, cotton swabs, bandages, then headed for the counter.

As Horace stood in line behind a ripe woman with scraggly blonde hair and a brood of plump boys groping at the chocolate bar rack and squalling for their fill, a revelation came, and he turned his cart around.

Horace found himself in the camping section. Something about the memory of the time he had spent with his family traversing the American West brought forth the idea of recreation. He would forgo the risk of hotels and become a wild man. He would retreat into the forest. Horace would camp and hunt inside dark groves, bathe and fish in shallow rivers. He would cascade the sand dunes of Nevada and sleep amongst the rattlesnakes in Idaho. He felt nature summoning him to its primal places. Visions of windswept valleys and dripping timbers filled his mind. He saw himself standing on the precipice of a rocky ridge, gazing across a plain of dirt and shrubs and desert flowers, at a full moon, a sprawl of infinite stars.

Horace was sixty-three, sure, but he figured himself capable of braving the elements. He was a man, after all, and a fighter. Untamed lands would not balk him, nor leave him defeated. Did people not wander terrain far harsher for thousands of years before the advent of houses and cities and cars? Why should Horace be less qualified to roam free than the savages of centuries past?

It was not his first time wanting to go rogue. Horace had contemplated an escape to the Northern Territories of Canada before, even Alaska, to spend his final years as a mountain man, basking in the glory of Mother Earth without the chatter of human kind to mar his fleeting existence. Now the opportunity was upon him. Horace would finally heed nature's call.

It was in America's lonely countryside that Horace vowed to find sanctuary. On barren shores and inside hushed woods, Horace Steeple would evade justice and seize a peaceful end. Not absolution or forgiveness, for he did not want either. He felt no guilt for the crime committed. He sought only refuge, and knew now where to seek it. Horace also knew that sometimes in life, the only way forward is to burn every bridge, scorch every trail, and stumble through the smoke to a better place.

As he stacked his cart full of supplies: tent, cooking gear, sleeping bag, lawn chair, air mattress, etc., he envisioned his family coming to visit him. One phone call and Lilly and Gloria could drag their husbands and Horace's grandchildren to see him on whatever plot of land he staked. He figured it would be their own rite of passage, cramped cars and endless swatches of highway. The notion excited Horace, and he hurried through the aisles, dumping item after item onto the growing mountain in his cart.

He was checking out the rifles in the hunting section when someone spoke to him and disrupted Horace's fantasy.

Carnivores

"Full load, hey? Spontaneous camping trip to Canada? Seen folk do it before. Awful cold up there, you know. I hear they ski all year 'round in some parts."

Horace laughed and turned his attention to the speaker, a Walmart employee not much younger than himself. She had curly black hair and wise green eyes, a squat, witchy frame. "No, miss," Horace said. "I've actually just left Canada. This is my first trip alone, eh. I'm thinking about going native."

"I see that," she said, pointing to his full cart. "Looks like you've got everything you need to vanish, and then some. If I didn't know any better, I'd peg you a man on the run. Er, maybe if you were a few years younger." She shot him a playful wink.

Horace grinned. "Are you calling me old?"

"Oh, no older than me." She walked around his cart to take her place behind the counter, rifles arranged on the wall behind her. "Afraid I can't offer up any of these guns, seeing as your Canadian and all. But these knives are available if you're in need of something sharp to carry into the woods."

"I do need a blade," Horace admitted. He tapped on the glass. "How about that Buck? Any good for skinning?"

Her eyes flashed to his wrist, to the watch peeking out of his sleeve. "What'll you be skinning, exactly?"

Horace looked down and realized he had missed something. Red specks dotted the silver band and the glass face of his watch. "Animals," he said, quickly hiding the time keeper under his sleeve. "That's it, animals and fish."

The two regarded each other with quiet knowing. Horace's heart beat in his chest and his throat became tight. The woman—a tag on her blue apron said her name was Mary—simply looked at him.

It was an odd thing, for an innocent person to stumble upon a guilty one, put together a small set of clues and allow their intuition to penetrate the guilty one's smiling facade. It was bad news for Horace. If Mary followed the instinct in her gut and picked up the phone, reported a suspicious character browsing the Walmart rifles with blood on his watch, Horace's dream of wooded seclusion and starry nights would be gone.

He thought for sure Mary would pick up the phone on the counter, transmit an SOS over the store's PA system, yet she did not. Mary said, "Well, the Buck'll cut through any ol' thing. Bone, wood, skin. I'd wager it the best tool a woodsman could carry."

Their eyes never went back to the knife, but remained locked. Horace was ready to run and abandon his supplies at the slightest hint of treachery, while Mary seemed to be studying his soul.

"I'll take it, thanks."

"Figured you would. Anything else?"

The charade was over. Mary knew he was hiding something. It was clear in her eyes. It was clear in how profusely Horace sweat. Best now to be honest. Mary appeared to see something in Horace that staved her from raising alarm.

"I need a truck," Horace said.

"Got cash?"

"Or trade. New for old."

"Any ol' truck?"

"One with plates would be appreciated."

"How far'll you be running?"

"Far."

She rolled her thin lips, mulling it over. "Wager you'll still be in town 'round six?"

Carnivores

"Time's not on my side. I'll need shelter come night fall."

Again, Mary rolled her lips and contemplated. She said, "Front doors, just after six. I'll help as best I can."

Horace nodded.

Then Mary's tone jumped a notch and she flashed Horace a toothy smile. "Box up the knife for you?"

The tense aura of negotiation was gone. Only now did Horace understand how deathly serious the Bellingham Walmart's hunting department had become in those few moments. The din of busy shoppers, squeaky wheels, and crying babies all came into focus, and Horace had to take a second to process the sudden cacophony before he replied. "Yes, please. Thank you very much, for everything."

Mary smiled. "Don't make me regret it, Mr."

6

He was parked near the main doors at six o'clock, just as the sun began to set. Horace had used the hours between to clean up and change. Inside a gas station washroom, Horace had scrubbed the blood off his watch, removed his leather gloves and tossed them in the garbage, disinfected and bandaged his cut-up hands, and traded his bloody clothes for new department store duds. He had thought about eating, but lacked an appetite.

As Horace waited for Mary to exit, or for the police to surround him, he pondered the reckless decision of returning to Walmart. It would have been easy for the helpful woman to turn around and call the authorities, report an old man from Canada stained with blood and fleeing into the wild. He hoped that was not the case. He hoped the kindness he glimpsed in Mary's eyes was genuine. Was it so hard to believe

15

there were still earnest people in the world? Was it so far fetched to think Mary could be a sincere human being, eager to help a man in need? Horace hoped not.

His concerns were laid to rest when Mary shuffled out of the automatic doors in her blue uniform. He recognized her impish figure and long curly hair, though he could not see her face due to a rapidly growing shadow in front of the store. She waited on the curb, looking for her stranger, and Horace started his engine and pulled around to meet her.

7

He had managed to fit all his supplies in the back cab and leave enough room in the front for Mary to climb in without sitting on anything.

"Didn't think you'd come," she said as Horace drove his black F-150 out of the parking lot and onto the road.

"Honestly," he said, chuckling, "neither did I. I was anticipating a task force to converge on me at any moment."

"Must've been a relief to see little ol' me stroll out the doors."

"That it was, Mary. It is Mary, right?"

"Going on fifty-five years now."

"My names Horace, has been for the last sixty-three."

"Oh." She looked surprised. "You *are* an old geezer. Good looking man for your age, though. Strong, healthy, lots of hair. Can color me impressed."

Horace smiled, turning onto the main thoroughfare through town. "You're quite the gem yourself, Mary. I would have thought you twenty years my younger."

"Oh, don't tease an ol' woman."

"Hush!" He cried, ever the gentleman. "Fifty-five is not old. I mean it. It's not every day I happen upon a kind young fox so willing to help a stranger."

"Call it intuition," Mary said. "Now listen, I don't know what you've gone and done in your country, nor why you're in mine, but I can't sense a single mean bone in your body. Far as I'm concerned, folk ought to help other folk in need if they're able. Now you say you need a truck and have the hard-earned cash to pay for it, and my late husband, Marcus, bless his soul, left his ol' beater sitting in the driveway. I reckon that'll do ya just fine."

"I appreciate it," Horace said. "Really, I do. If I had never met you today, I don't know what might have become of me. You saved my life, Mary."

"Be sure not to tell anyone," she said, smiling.

They turned and grinned at one another in perfect harmony, and something stirred inside Horace. A thing that he had not felt since the passing of Susan. He thought Mary felt it too, for he glimpsed more than warmth in her smile, and had the distinct sensation of something beyond mere cordiality in the way she looked at him.

8

Mary lived outside town, closer to Laurel than to Bellingham. She directed Horace north along Guide Meridian, then right onto East Axton Road. They chatted and flirted in a way that seemed new to them both, one being a widow and the other a widower. It was refreshing. Mary and Horace felt comfortable in each other's company, which the old boxer had not expected. His deeds never came into question, nor the bandages plastered over his hands. Horace, in turn, never asked Mary how she managed the six-mile journey to and from work every day without a car, or what happened to her husband.

For Horace, it had been one hell of a day. In less than ten hours he had killed three men, fled his country, and was driving into the middle of nowhere, Washington State, with a semi-attractive stranger. He could not have wished for a better start to his adventure, nor a more suitable way to rejuvenate his spirit.

They drove past farms and old dilapidated sheds, the shadows of night beginning to envelop patches of timber, blacken fields and turn ditches into dark gullies. Horace drove slowly, trying to prolong their conversation before they arrived at her home and talk turned to business. He caught sight of a fence on the road's left side that led to a quarry, which Mary had mentioned earlier, some run-down excavation site where youngsters go to drink beer and fuck. As they passed the gate, Horace spotted a pair of dark figures dancing beyond its steel links.

They gave Horace the creeps, made him shudder. He checked his rear-view mirror but they were gone. He dismissed the twirling shades as workers ending their day, the darkness deceiving Horace's old, fragile mind.

Mary said, "Take a right at the next intersection."

"Okie doke."

Horace took a right on Hannegan Road and drove on until Mary signaled for him to turn right down a driveway. His truck barely fit below a canopy of trees that made the entrance almost invisible in the deepening dusk.

The house was surprisingly large. It was more like a farm. There was a shed next to the home and a collection of rusted cars near it, an unbreakable wall of trees beyond. The whole property was bordered by tall green timbers, the house itself segregated from the massive yard by smaller trees and bushes, a fortress guarded by a barricade of greenery.

Horace parked next to an old Chevrolet and Mary said, "That there is Marcus' ol' Chevy. And that's the house we were supposed to grow old together in. Looks like I'll be the only one doing the growing. Still, I keep her clean and tidy and the spare bedroom ready for guests, even though my dear Sherman went off to fight the Muslims and hasn't come home yet. Poor boy. I sure hope he sends them all to Hell."

Mary let out a sad, tired sigh. "But that's a story for another time. Now, I reckon we've some business. You fixing to eat, Horace? I haven't cooked for anyone in an age. I could fry up something if you want while you take the ol' Chevy out for a spin, make sure she still purrs, just like Marcus used to like."

Horace turned off the engine, appearing years younger in the glow of the buttons and dials on the dashboard. He said, "If you're offering me a home cooked meal, who am I to refuse? That sounds just great, Mary. Thank you. I'll drive to town and back, fill the truck up with gas and make sure everything checks out, then be back in time to taste your cooking."

"Sounds fine to me. Just let me grab the keys from inside and you'll be on your way. Take your time, as it'll be an hour or so till supper. You can sleep in the guest room, then head off again in the morning, less you're wanting to drive on through the night."

9

Horace shut the door to Marcus' ol' Chevy and sighed. The world outside was black, the porchlight a beacon in the gloom of foliage and shadows. He adjusted his seat, then the mirrors as best he could in the dark and tried the key.

The truck groaned to life and the headlights shone a beam across the driveway to the shed and the rusted cars. He thought he saw an animal scurry from the light, maybe a raccoon, but he was unsure.

Horace reversed out of the driveway and took a left on Hannegan Road, figuring to retrace his path back to Bellingham. The truck ran just fine. It was not that old, less than ten years. The glowing odometer read 40,000 miles, which made Horace wonder how long ago Marcus had passed on, and how many years the truck had sat idle.

Horace revved the engine and allowed the truck's power to whisk him past large plots of land masked in darkness. He turned left at the first intersection onto East Axton Road. As he did, the radio activated on its own and a country singer's voice blared out of the speakers, nearly giving Horace a heart attack.

"Jesus." His heart lurched into his throat. "Stupid old machine." Horace searched for the power button, found the knob and pressed it, ushering silence back into the cab. Flustered, Horace set his eyes back on the road—then screamed.

"Oh god!"

Two people stood in the middle of the lane, hand in hand. They were dim and Horace could not see their faces, so ghostly they could have been a mirage. He glimpsed only the outline of their unflinching bodies before he jerked the wheel and the truck swerved into the ditch. Horace hit the brakes and skidded to halt six inches from a cluster of trees.

He sat there, gripping the wheel tight in both hands, his breath short and quick. The engine thrummed beneath him. Its constant rumble bore into his body until his temper flared and he screamed and smashed his fists against the wheel.

"What in the name of God were they thinking, standing in the middle of the road like that? Were they trying to get themselves killed? Because that's a real good way to go about it!"

Horace was wild. He looked up at the branches scratching the windshield, begging to get in. He looked out his window and saw the two obscure figures lingering above the ditch he had driven into, hand in hand, watching him.

"No, don't help the old man. Don't go see if he's okay. Why bother? You shits. You little shits!"

He slammed the truck into park and opened his door, left the vehicle running and staggered out onto the grass, calling after them, "What the hell are you doing?"

The faceless did not answer. They skipped up a gravel road, towards the same gate Horace had drove by earlier, where he had witnessed those opaque individuals in celebration of the night.

He abandoned the truck and hiked up the ditch, along the country road to the gravel drive. When Horace looked up the way, he saw that the two figures had moved beyond the gate and stood frigid, looking at him.

"Get back here!"

They seemed to laugh at his rage, though he heard no sound. Horace was helplessly as they ignored him, turned and skipped off in the direction of the quarry, their ambiguous forms coalescing with the dark world.

Consumed by anger, Horace followed.

10

He lost track of the mysterious twins the moment he made it over the gate, which only made him angrier. Horace marched awkwardly inside muddy ruts and the tracks made by heavy machines, deeper into the reservoir's creepy void.

"Where are you, damnit?"

Everything Horace saw was a dim copy of itself. Piles of gravel were towering mounds of coal. Idle dump trucks were reduced to hollow shells, pieces of equipment with chutes and ladders and tall platforms like the bones of prehistoric beasts.

He knew the shades could be lurking anywhere in that midnight playground, and after a while of following the ruts in the disturbed ground Horace's anger settled and his determination died. He had walked a considerable distance into the field of indiscriminate things and a vulnerable feeling now overcame him.

Horace made the decision to retreat. He had become crushed by the night's imposing weight and paranoid of its depths. H turned to flee, only to find himself blocked by the two people he had been chasing. Only, they were not people. They were silhouettes, as vague and dark as everything else.

With his fury abated and his courage corrupted by the dread of a starless night, Horace was left intimidated by the ghosts, unnerved by how their crepuscular forms wavered and blended with the air.

"Keep away," he told them. "I don't want to kill anyone else today. Not if I don't have to."

Horace's threat sounded weak, even to him. The pair began to approach, floating across the ground.

He forfeited all pride and ran. Horace left the track and sprinted towards the safety of a group of buildings down hill from him, what looked to be a lost village of ramshackle huts at the bottom of a dune.

Half way down it he fell. Horace tripped and

rolled painfully in an avalanche of pebbles and lost his glasses in the torrent. When he stood up, he could see nothing. The darkness that had limited his perception was now total.

There was a reservoir a few meters from him, its surface a pan of black ice. But Horace could not see it. The buildings he had sought shelter in were a blur in his vision. He certainly did not see the shades, the countless shadows that crept from the derelict structures; rose from the inky lake; emerged from piles of rock like buried dead and even materialized from the darkness itself.

But he could feel their encroaching presence. Horace shouted and flailed as icy fingers seized his arms and legs, grasped his head and tugged on his ears, tore at his useless eyes. He screamed and they poured into his mouth. It was terrible, like runny tar flowing down his throat and blackening in his insides.

11

When Horace came to, he was back behind the wheel of Marcus' ol' Chevy, a little dazed. The engine still ran, chugging away. He gave his head a shake and lurched the truck into reverse, maneuvered out of the ditch and drove back to Mary's house.

12

The welcoming aroma of seasoned potatoes and marinated pork greeted Horace in the foyer. He removed his dirty sneakers and called out, "Mary, where are you, dear?"

"In here."

He made his way through the house in pursuit of her voice, admiring the quaint artifacts and ancient portraits displayed throughout Mary's home, the old fashion furniture and the homey aura of the place. He found Mary in the kitchen. The table was set for two, glasses and a bottle of wine center between a pair of plates overflowing with potatoes and vegetables and succulent pork chops. The smell made his mouth water.

Horace said, "Smells terrific, Mary. I can't believe you went through all this trouble for me. I would have been happy with your company and a loaf of bread."

"Oh, no trouble at all," she said from her station at the sink. "I was starting to think I'd be eating alone, and that you'd run off. Took your time, I'd say. It's nearly 10 o'clock."

Horace had never even checked the time. His head still hurt from his tumble down the gravel mountain, though he blamed his headache on the crash, on hitting the steering wheel. Horace had no memory of the taunting shadows or his midnight pursuit.

"Funny story," he said. "There were people in the road and I had to swerve to avoid them. I drove straight into the ditch, Mary. Hand to God, I did. The crash must have knocked me out longer than I thought."

Mary turned from the bubbles and dirty dishes and gasped at the sight of Horace. He had a deep, bleeding gash in his head. "By God's grace, Horace. Your head, It's bleeding. Are you alright? Is anything broken?"

"No, I feel fine." He touched the throbbing spot on his head and his fingers came away wet. "But I must have wacked my noggin pretty damn hard."

"I'd say." Mary rushed over to him, took Horace gently by the arm. "Come into the wash, sweetheart. Let's get you cleaned up."

13

"What happened to the people you saw in the road?"

Mary asked. She had Horace on the toilet lid, dabbing at the blood leaking from the fissure in his skull.

"They must have run off."

"Teenagers," she said with a scowl. "Probably some kids mucking around in the old quarry. They go missing, you know. At least once a moon some kid's face gets plastered all over the billboard at work, gone missing up there near the quarry."

"Could be, Mary. Could be."

She threw her cotton swab into the wastebasket and grabbed a new one, continued to dab the blood off Horace's head. "Strange," she said. "I thought your blood was black because it's such a deep wound. But it really is black. It's like you're bleeding tar, darling."

Horace was having a hard time. He could not focus. He had become fascinated by the shape of Mary's breasts through the fabric of her sweater. "Yeah... tar." He was imagining the softness of the wool against Mary's delicate nipples. The thought made him hard. Which was odd, because Horace's libido had dried-up a few years ago, and now on Mary's toilet it flared to life in a violent and insistent way. He watched her chest heave as she cleaned his wound.

"Your blood is so black. Are you sure you're alright?"

"Yeah. I'm alright." And he could feel the weight of them in his hands, the silk of her flesh, how her breasts squished when he squeezed, how they pushed together and how her nipples hardened in Horace's mouth, how he circled them with his tongue, then swallowed and sucked.

Horace's eyes drooped as the heat mounted in his loins, a toxic fire spreading from toes to fingers, to his very eyeballs. It trickled like drips of magma to Horace's core, igniting him in a way that made him savage.

Mary noticed the deranged look of him. "Feeling woozy, darling?"

"Feeling..." His voice was distant, dreamy.

"Darling, you might have a concussion." Mary lifted Horace's chin and looked in his eyes. Her breath caught in her throat. "By God's love! Your eyes are gone black. Horace, dear, you need a hospital right away. Looks like tadpoles swimming through the whites of your eyes, taking over."

"Yes, taking over..."

Mary gazed into his face with sympathy and concern, but all Horace could see were her lips, thin and parted and cracked and waxy with red lipstick. He needed them. He needed to taste them, to feel them on his skin. He needed her mouth to fill and drip with his saliva, and for their tongues to intertwine.

Horace lunged forward and kissed her, grabbed Mary's face in his powerful hands and jammed his tongue into her mouth. She tried to pull away, but Horace rose from the toilet and they stumbled back until Mary crashed into the wall.

"I need you," he said, sliding one hand to her breast while smothering her face with the other.

Mary was aghast. "No, darlin'. It's not right. You're in need of help. You're not right in your head. You've been injured."

Horace moaned and squeezed Mary's breasts, bit her neck like the animal he had become, thrusting his rigid cock against her bladder.

"I mean it." Mary was on the verge of tears, unable to gather the courage to flee or fight, feeling trapped. "I don't want it, ya hear. I don't."

"*Yesss*," he hissed. "I want it."

Horace stood a giant next to Mary, a wall she

could not pass. His muscles bulged sickly beneath his sweater and the veins of his neck and forehead were distended, his eyes orbs of churning pitch, the crevice on his skullcap bubbling and belching inky goo.

Mary started to cry. Tears streamed down her cheeks and she trembled. The stranger she had welcomed so warmly into her home huffed in her ear like a feral beast, forced up her arms and pulled her sweater over her head.

Mary shuddered against the wall, her large, sagging breasts bare and her wild black hair draped over her shoulders. The seething man lifted one of her teats to his mouth and indulged with feverish zeal. She wept in shame as he turned her around and pressed her face against the wall, heaving as primal creatures do. Horace loosened his belt and dropped his pants. Mary cringed, knowing what was about to happen and too scared to stop it. She whimpered when Horace helped himself to her insides. He inserted his blood engorged cock into the poor woman and grunted, dead eyes turned to the ceiling.

That was it. One pump and the brutality was over. Mary's cries were stifled by the inky semen that flowed into her body and dribbled down her leg, black cum slithering down her thigh.

14

Horace and Mary ate a cold dinner of potatoes and pork. Mostly they flirted. They were more like shy teenagers than grown folk with children of their own. It was the same as earlier in the truck, the same timid friendliness, joking and laughing while Horace complimented Mary's cooking. Neither of them mentioned Horace's assault in the toilet. They had already forgotten it.

When the meal was finished, Horace helped Mary wash up. After the kitchen was clean, the couple retreated to Mary's bedroom. She held his hand and guided him through the hallway and onto her bed. And that was where they ravaged each other. Horace had not felt so sexually explosive since his twenties. Mary was a minx. She sucked Horace and let him bend her in half. She begged for Horace to fuck her like a slave and spit in her face. It was horrendous, the spirit of deviance that possessed these two wholesome people. They devoured each other unto the dawn.

When the first rays of daylight peeked through the blinds, Horace and Mary curled beneath the blankets and shivered. They stayed that way until the night, when darkness once more laid claim to the world. Then Mary packed a bag of odds and ends, clothes and such, and climbed into the passenger seat of her deceased husband's truck.

"Ready?" Horace asked, smiling behind the wheel.

Mary turned sparkling green eyes on him. "Course. Ready as can be."

Horace chuckled and slipped the truck into reverse. They left behind Mary's lifetime home and embraced an empty stretch of blacktop. Horace navigated towards I-5, driving past buildings wreathed in twilight, barren fields like patches of void space and somber trees that concealed dense, lightless forests.

Carnivores

KATELYN, THE PURE

PURE, RAVENOUS HUNGER

1

"No, I...

"Yes.

"Okay.

"But I have schoo--

"I know, Mamma, I know. But Sacramento is what, two-thousand miles away?

"Yeah, yeah. I know where I live. I was exaggerating, Mamma, you--

"Yeah.

"Yes. Yes, Mamma. I'll figure it out. But I've gotta run. I'll--

"No, I *do* want to talk, but Mamma, I gotta go.

"Yeah, love you too. Bye."

Katelyn sighed and hung up the phone.

"Mamma bear on the line?"

"No, Ash. It was Jay-Z. He wants me to drive from Denver to Sacramento, so I can be one of his back up dancers."

"Oh, snap! Congratulations, Katy baby. They'll probably give you one of those golden bikinis and get you to shake your fat black tits in front of the camera for the whole nation to see. What an accomplishment. But wait, are you up on your twerking?"

Katelyn sighed, eyes glued to her phone as her and Ashley walked along the Campus Green, north towards E. Asbury Avenue in pursuit of an early evening drink. "Yes, Ashley, my twerk is on point."

"As it should be. You're a student of law, Kate, in your second year at the University of Denver Law School. If you don't know how to twerk by now, you never will. I mean, how do you expect to win a single case without giving the judge a little of that bouncy-bouncy." Ashley throttled her hips into Katelyn, near knocking the girl over, then bounced her ass off her friend. "Twerk, twerk, twerk!"

Katelyn almost dropped her phone she laughed so hard. Her and Ashley butt-checked each other until their laughing boiled and died and they continued along the dirt path, giggling.

"So, what did she want?" Ashley asked.

"For me to come home. What else? It's not like she ever calls just to chat. Never just phones to see how I'm doing, how my grades are, if I have any boys in my life."

"Like you ever do. When does she want you to visit?"

"Now."

"Now? Are you f-ing kidding me, Kate? She knows you have classes to go to, right? Like really, really important classes."

"She knows I have class, but she doesn't understand. Mamma never finished high school. She doesn't have a clue what it's like here; the pressure, our timetables, the stress, the professors breathing down our necks. She has no clue. Not one. Mamma thinks university is a breeding ground for rich kids to get high on designer drugs, party naked and wake up pregnant."

"Isn't it, though?"

The girls had reached the intersection of Asbury and University Blvd. They stopped and Katelyn gave Ashley a harsh look. "Maybe a bit. Like twenty-five, forty percent. But for people like you and I who didn't grow up knowing we were destined for law school. Let me repeat that: *Laaaw-schooool.* For us, it's more than fun and parties. It's our only chance. Mamma will never see that."

Carnivores

"That's her loss, Katy baby. Now look, are we gonna stand in front of the Conoco all day, or can we finish this conversation inside? I've had a bullshit day and I'd love a beer."

"Yeah, yeah. Let's go."

2

The Crimson and Gold Tavern was Katelyn and Ashley's long-established hideout. When the girls were too lazy to drive some place exciting and neither wanted to go home to their miserable, overcrowded apartments, they made the five-minute trek from campus to the tavern for drinks. The staff knew their faces and their names, and the place was never too hectic that they had to scream over a choir of other voices to be heard; though on occasion, and later in the evening, the thirsty savages did mass in great numbers.

On that Tuesday in May there were only two groups of students seated inside, sipping drinks and complaining about whatever ungodly tasks their professors had assigned them.

Katelyn and Ashley waved and said hello to Blaze, the lanky guy behind the bar, and walked out to the patio to enjoy some warmth and tranquility.

"You know, Kate, this is like our home away from home away from home," Ashley said. "We escaped our lives to start fresh in Colorado, and now we can't stomach our homes, so we sit in this place and bitch. Bitch, bitch, bitch."

"I prefer the term: *discuss*," Katelyn said. "We are *discussing* the aspects of our lives which we find distasteful, and those around us who we find...*tedious.*"

Ashley glared across the table. "So, you're some kind a' fancy bitch?"

"I prefer the term *fancy bitch extraordinaire,* thank you very much."

"How about, *her royal bitchness?*" Came the chipper voice of Blaze. He strolled across the patio, grinning a dumb grin, his eyes dancing over Katelyn with so much enthusiasm she could almost feel his cock jamming against her hip. "I think it has quite the ring to it," he said.

"Me too," Ashley said. She flashed Katelyn a teasing smirk, eyes gleaming devilishly behind her massive shades.

"Thanks, Blaze," Katelyn said. "Maybe you can find me a crown."

"Yeah, su--"

"But until then, we would like two beers. Thank you."

"Of course, Kate. Two cold ones for my two favorite law students, coming right up."

Blaze clearly wanted to linger, but the giggles rising out of Ashley and the apparent look of indifference on Katelyn's face, her dark eyes staring angrily at her friend, made Blaze depart.

Ashley burst into laughter.

"Shut up," Katelyn said. "Don't even say it. Say it, and you can walk your black ass home."

Ashley could not help herself. "Just do it, Kate. You know he wants it. He was hard as a rock the moment we walked in. I think I saw his boner trying to break free of his jeans."

"Shut up."

"Just take him home. Stop making the poor boy wonder. Give him a glimpse of those luscious twins. Let him have a feel, Katy baby!"

"I swear to god, Ash, I am going to pour my beer over your head and leave."

"Oh, relax. I'm just teasing. If Blaze wasn't such a fuckboy, I would take him off your hands myself.

He's not terrible looking. Kind a' scrawny."

Katelyn rolled her eyes. "You know he'd still eye-rape me. You could ride him all night long, the skinny whore would still hound me the next day."

"You know what, Katelyn Griffin? I'd say that--"

The sound of Blaze's footsteps crossing the patio stopped Ashley mid-sentence. "Two beers for two beautiful girls," he said, planting a pair of bottles on the table. "Anything else?"

"Katelyn here was hoping--"

"Your fucking mouth, Ashley Johnston!"

Blaze grinned back and forth between them, thinking he was on the brink of something long awaited. His grin vanished when Katelyn looked up at him and said, "No, that will be all. Go man your station. Thank you."

Ashley broke into another giggle fit as Blaze sauntered back inside the tavern, defeated.

"Why do you have to do this every time?" Katelyn asked.

"Because it's funny and I like it."

Kate sighed and took a sip of her beer. "Well it's annoying. If I see a boy I like, I can pick him up myself, thanks."

"Oh yeah? When will that be? I've known you a long time now, Katy baby, and I haven't seen you pick a man up. Not ever. I've seen a devil's horde chase your sweet ass. I've seen men stumble head over foot to try and get a whiff of those long curly locks, or a peek at your goodies, but never have I seen one reach home. Not even first."

"Because I keep my sexual endeavors to myself, unlike some people who broadcast their promiscuity over the loud speakers."

Ashley gasped. "You bitch!" Then smiled. "I like the attention."

"You do. I don't."

"Yes, but that's why we make such a great team."

Ashley extended her beer and the girls clinked glasses. "True enough," Katelyn said.

They got cozy in their chairs, enjoyed the sun on their skin while they sipped cold beer. They let the silence fall over them and slipped into thought. Katelyn began to wonder why she lied to her friend.

3

It was nothing sinister. She was not in the least bit gay. Not even curious. Katelyn had no sick fetishes. No odd sexual compulsions. Katelyn Griffin was merely a virgin. Nothing obscene or degrading about that; perhaps a little embarrassing, but Ashley would not have cared. She would have taunted Katelyn without mercy until the end of days. Ridicule and mockery would be in ample supply until they withered, grew old, and died. But never would Ashley have cared, nor judged her friend for her abstinence.

In fact, there was no reason behind Katelyn's chastity. She had met guys she liked. She had kissed boys. She had even touched James McDonald's penis when she was eighteen, a year before impeccable grades and a fiery ambition would bestow her with an all expenses paid residency at the University of Denver to pursue a career in law—though she refused to put it in her mouth. He asked. Well, more like begged, but she denied him, and after her hand was sticky with his spunk and James buckled up his pants and resumed watching TV like nothing had happened, Katelyn felt disgusted. She washed her hands and when James left, never talked to him again.

Of course, being who she was, Katelyn had a myriad of suitors to choose from, all eager to escort her on a *"magical"* date. They promised shiny things and fast cars, dinners at five-star restaurants and trips to the Bahamas.

None of the boys where Katelyn had grown up—the greasy neighborhood of Meadowview, South Sacramento—could have offered any of those things on the best of days. Their idea of a romantic date was a trip in their mom's beat up car to a conspicuous place so Katelyn could suck their dick from the passenger seat while bums foraged in the alley for bottles. That nonsense never worked when she was a teenager, and as a young adult, she never accepted the propositions of her classmates, though they were certainly more appealing.

And so, Katelyn Griffin kept her virginity. She was a gorgeous woman with chestnut eyes and curly black hair, a body so firm and ebony and voluptuous that the humble of men would have resorted to the lowest and most pathetic of means to catch a glimpse of her in a bikini—and a virgin.

"So?" Ashley said, breaking the silence.

"So what?"

"Are you going home, back ta tha hood, sista?"

Katelyn frowned. She hated when Ashley used her stupid ghetto accent.

"Yeah, I think so. Mamma says she's sick. Like, really sick this time. Apparently, the hospital won't let her leave. Nick is there everyday."

"Your brother?"

"Yes."

"I thought he was in jail? Didn't he get caught selling crack or some shit?"

"Mhm. Got out a month ago. I don't care what Nick does. He's my brother and I love him in the same way I love Mamma, but other than that...." Katelyn sighed. "Other than that, I don't care what they do with their lives."

"Cold as ice, Katy."

"Yeah, well, Nick and I were raised under the same roof. We went to the same school, had the same opportunities, same teachers. Why am I in Denver on my way to becoming a lawyer and my stupid brother is hanging out on Stockton Boulevard selling crack?"

"Tits?"

"Shut up, Ashley. Everything is tits with you. My tits didn't get me this far. My brain did. Nick's brain just never evolved. If you ask me, my brother is a no-good street thug and he'll die under a bridge somewhere or get stabbed to death in Folsom State. For Christ's sake, Ash, the only time he calls me is when he needs legal advice. It's pathetic and I just don't care. I made this my life and I left all that shit behind. I'll go see Mamma to rest and be done with it."

Ashley withheld her witty response. It was one of the few times she recognized her friend's upset and the seriousness of the subject matter. She took a long drink and sighed.

"I understand," Ashley said. "My family's the same. Same trouble. Same colors. Different state. Only mine are proud of me, rather than angry about me leaving them. They're still a pack of dirt bag junkies and gang bangers, but they *are* proud. I still feel like one of the family when I visit."

Ashley took a long drink, looked sadly at the table and said, "It's not the leaving that's hard, you know. For me, it's the staying away. The past always tries to sneak up and drag me back to where I came from. Memories and familiarity want to impede my progress, something internal telling me to go home and revert into the brat I was, and everyone knew I would grow to be. It's tough to block out that instinct and look ahead. I think, in part, because it's harder to stay in this school and work and focus on life than it is to drop out and go home and get pregnant and work at the fucking Walmart."

"Orpheus and Eurydice," Katelyn said.

"Who?"

"Greek mythology, Ash. Orpheus lost his wife, Eurydice, to a snake bite, and went to the underworld to retrieve her. He played his lyre for Hades and Persephone, and the god of the underworld felt pity for him. Hades agreed to let Eurydice follow him back to the world of the living on one condition: She would follow, and he would not look back. If he did, she would be lost to the stygian abyss forever."

"You're such a nerd," Ashley said, smiling. "So, what happened?"

"Well, Orpheus lost patience and looked behind him, untrusting of Hades. Sure enough, his wife's shade had been following silently behind, but once his eyes fell upon Eurydice, she was whisked back into the depths of Tartarus."

Ashley finished her beer and belched in a rather crude fashion, then said, "So, what you're saying is you need to look forward and have faith, and if you look in reverse, your whole life can slip away."

Katelyn thought, finished her beer and said, "Exactly. Don't let worry or concern turn you around. Don't lose sight of the future."

"Spoken like a true woman of law. Critical and heartless. I love it. Now quick, here comes Blaze. Maybe, just maybe, if you ask real nice, you can fuck him in the bathroom."

4

"Got everything you need?"

"Yup."

"Tell Mrs. Einstein you're going to be gone a

few days?"

"Yup."

"How'd she take it?"

"Oh god, she doesn't care about me. It upsets me more than her."

"Ever the machine."

"Mhm."

Katelyn tossed her suitcase into the trunk of her car and gave Ashley a hug. "See you in a few," she said, then walked to the driver's side and climbed in.

Ashley waved and Katelyn drove off, eager to be done with what she hoped would be her last visit to Sacramento.

It was eleven-hundred miles. She would drive through Salt Lake City, over a long stretch of nothingness, into Reno, then home. She figured three days to get there, one to say her goodbyes, and three to travel back. She could study along the way and catch up on whatever work she missed upon her return. No sweat.

An hour of creeping through Denver's hustle and bustle brought Katelyn to the freeway. Soon after, the sprawl of civilization began to shrink in her rear-view mirror, and so too did her stress. All her anxieties faded and lost grip and she calmed for the first time in a long time. Narrow city lanes twisted and met and grew large, poured as streams into the great river known as I70, and Katelyn's dour mood washed away in the current of west flowing cars. The sun beamed down from a blue and cloudless sky, and all in the distance rose mountains to breach that open air. On the radio blared a tune. It was a classic, "*On the Road Again,*" and it was not long before the mixture of melody and scenery and brightness and the comfortable cavity of her car conjured a sensation of freedom, a sort of liberation that comes only to those lone wanderers on the open road.

It was a first for Kate, who was a stranger to long journeys. Her previous trips between Denver and Sacramento had been on an airplane. Now she had a little black car. It was a new addition in Katelyn Griffin's ever prosperous life, and she had yet to utilize the machine for anything beyond city driving, the occasional jaunt to Boulder.

Now she raced along the interstate, Earth's glory to behold, leagues of highway to pursue, and that shocking revelation thrust itself upon her without warning. All at once she understood the thrill of endless terrain, the adventure of unexplored valleys, and the erotic mystery of every anonymous face outside the window. In an instant, the world peeled and flayed and opened in a gesture of unconditional welcome, and Kate embraced it—rushed towards it with a grin on her dark virgin lips and reveries of the undiscovered dancing romantically behind her eyes.

5

A whirlwind of fantasy blew through Katelyn's head in the two hours between Denver and her surrender to the earthly fascination that took shape during those miles of road. She tried to resist, but it was no good. She broke. Her will crumbled and compulsion claimed her senses. She became claustrophobic, anxious to leave the car. Katelyn searched for road signs, for any clue, any direction that would lead her to an outpost from which to view the world. She wished to behold the lush mountain splendor she drove through from a high vantage, unobstructed and untainted, if only for a minute.

Vail, Colorado. She had heard the town's name in passing, in the halls of her university. She knew it was a popular winter destination among students and that they flocked to Vail Mountain's impressive ski resort. She knew it was flanked on all sides by rolling hills and deep woods, lakes and creeks. As the quaint little village approached on the left of the interstate, she knew it to be the place where she would find her path into the wilderness.

Katelyn left I70 and entered the town. She hugged the cute little roundabout that marked Vail's entrance and continued down the main drag. She observed the old fashion shops and restaurants that lined the street, all those store windows advertising huge sales for outdoor gear and hiking equipment, the dinners promising an authentic taste of little America. Katelyn grinned at the utter perfection of the place; a North American Whoville. Folk walked the sidewalks with smiles and bags of groceries stacked flawlessly in their arms. They smiled and said good afternoon as they passed one another, and no one seemed to carry a single burden. People stopped at cross-walks and waved through their windows at the joyful children skipping across the road. Shopkeepers swept non-existent dust away from their doorways and patrons greeted them warmly. It was all very utopian, which made Katelyn feel that much more at home—that much more on the right path.

She found the visitors center and parked her car in the empty lot. The air that hit her face as she exited the vehicle was so refreshing that she lingered a moment, half in the car and half out, and basked in the freshness of it. Then she strolled over to a rack of free pamphlets beside the building's front door.

Katelyn turned the rack and snatched a few leaflets that looked interesting, then returned to her car where she scrutinized them one by one on the hood. There were adverts for skiing, hiking, horse back riding, river rafting, and two dozen dinning options. She folded up the useless promotions and inspected a guide to Vail's hiking trails.

"Gore Creek Trail," she whispered to herself. "Five point four eight miles.... Elevation of 11,390 feet... Spruce and fir forest... Alpine tundra to Gore Lake."

"Perfect!" She exclaimed, folding the pamphlet up with the rest.

Katelyn got in her car and started the engine, retreated out of town and down the highway to exit 180, breaking every speed limit in the process. From the exit, she followed a paved road to a not so paved road, then arrived in a region of tall spruce trees and vacant camping stalls. Katelyn saw only one R.V in Gore Creek Campground, but the occupants of that shabby thing were no where to be found. She parked at the trailhead, gathered up her things and got out.

She stood there looking at the trail's entrance, black purse slung over one shoulder, her enormous shades on the brim of her nose. She noted the rut of dirt that marked the path, traced it into the aspen grove where it eventually blended with the chaotic floor of rock and mud and broken sticks. Then she was off, gone into the shady wood.

Perhaps it was because Katelyn refused to watch horror films, or maybe the time just seemed irrelevant. Perhaps the idea of embarking on a five-and-a-half-mile hike into foreign territory while the sun crested the trees and nighttime waited just out of sight did not strike Katelyn as dangerous. Or, maybe she was unaware of those things, and ventured blind and ignorant into the forest.

6

Katelyn followed the earthen trail through a maze of dark green trees and strolled happily beside Gore

Creek with the sound of gushing water and restless birds all that was heard in that forest. She stopped to take pictures of the blue and white liquid sloshing in its gully and gawked upwards at the gray and brown slopes of the valley walls. She moved easily through meadows of tall grass, plains of fallen trees and discarded logs, white boulders jutting like half-buried dominos from the soft ground. She saw squirrels and birds by the dozen, and she saw the sun brighten and fall to a level that cast shadows behind her and created pockets of black beneath uprooted trees like the cruel bunkers of forest witches.

Katelyn reckoned to be on mile four. The path forked and one direction led to Gore Lake while the other went over Red Buffalo Pass. She veered left to reach the lake, and as she turned, realized she had lost the light.

Panic struck a gong in Kate's chest. She had somehow continued to walk through the timber fields without noticing the rise of night, and now it loomed total in every direction. She looked about and saw shadows moving discreetly amongst dark foliage like mischievous ghouls playing in the brush. She told herself it was the rustle of branches, nothing more. She told herself the haunted sounds emanating from the stark land were perpetrated by plants and evening animals, nothing more.

Katelyn dug deep in her purse and retrieved her phone. It was half past seven. She did the math on her fingers to try and calculate how long it took her to reach that fork in the road. At minimum, she had moved one mile each hour. That meant four hours to escape. Her phone blinked at 10 percent and Katelyn promptly shut it off, just in case.

She looked up the way, at the path that

ascended a vague hill with trees sparse here and there and rocks that looked like missing plots of reality in the pitch. The trail vanished within the obscurity of all that darkness and beyond were a few meager stars to illuminate the gloom and make it visible enough to be afraid.

Katelyn's heart fluttered at the immensity of the black. She no longer wished to pursue the path. She fled. She turned heel and galloped back the way she came, back into the thickness of the wood.

7

Her feet pounded the dirt and her purse jostled against her hip. Soon Katelyn's lungs were on fire and she had a horrible cramp. Yet Katelyn refused to stop for fear of the shadows.

All in the hollow of that scape were shadows that crept and lumbered bow-legged and tall and some short and all generated from some obsidian gunk or mutated from the vilest slime of Hell. They ran at stride with Katelyn and their voices were the wind. They blocked the path ahead until she closed enough distance and then they were never there at all, faded like ghosts. She turned once to glance behind her, and to Kate's horror there was a phalanx of shadows without faces following her down the trail. Their feet never lifted and they glided as a platoon of spectres through the wood.

She had to take a break. Her lungs were on fire and self preservation could no longer keep her feet in motion. Katelyn halted and dropped to her knees, and in that same instance the din of all those shadows died and in its stead was utter stillness. Not even the forest breathed. Katelyn huffed and puffed and swallowed dryly, the whole world spinning, her guts churning. She swung her purse onto the ground and fumbled for her phone, finding it and holding the power button. All around her night fiends and disfigured shadows of men and beasts and all manner of horrible things encroached.

Kate's phone booted on and the little jingle played. She tried to dial 911 but had no service there in that primal place. She instead activated the phone's flashlight and shone it out before her where every shifting form evaporated silently in the light.

She rose and began to walk, clutching her cramped side and using the phone's light as a beacon, a lighthouse beam sweeping over dark water, her blade of light cutting across the vague forest and disintegrating the shadows that stalked her like vampires in the sun.

It worked for some time and she managed to catch her breath. Katelyn figured to be half way back. Without stopping to ogle and with the initial boost granted by her mad dash, she knew it was not far to her car.

Then her phone died. It beeped and the light vanished. Phantasms sprouted from the ground like ethereal zombies. They descended from branches and rolled down hills, all their forms darker than the night itself.

"No, no, no." Katelyn shut her eyes against the impossible army. "This isn't happening. It's not real. No way. I'm stuck in the woods and I'm paranoid. That's all. I'm going to count to three. When I reach three, I'll open my eyes and everything will be fine.

"One.

"Two.

"Three."

8

Katelyn stumbled out of the woods dishevelled, seemingly emerged from a holocaust that blackened the world. Her car sat as it had in the lot and she staggered to it, a messy caricature of a few hours past. Her hair was untamed and her almond eyes held the same wild nature to them, scared but unsure why. Katelyn Griffin looked like the victim of a nocturnal predator, jeans torn and checkered blouse tattered as if by some elusive animal's claws, buttons ripped off and her breasts hoisted from of a rip in her tank top, the purple of her bra stained black with blood and blood seeping through other tears in her garments.

Katelyn reached her car and fumbled in her purse for the keys. She got in and started the engine, stared blankly ahead at the patch of forest that now appeared so ominous in the headlights, then spun the vehicle around. As she drove out of Gore Creek Campground, Katelyn saw again the R.V sitting idle in its lot, still lacking any sign of life, the camper dark and eerie and bound for decay. She wondered how many motorhomes lay abandoned across the nation, what parlor trick of shadows and spooks lured the owners off into the night, never to return, and how many of those godforsaken machines sat rusting in a junkyard while the humans that once drove them sat rotting in the woods.

9

Heading west along the interstate once more, Katelyn turned on the radio and calmed at the soothing sound of, "*Buffalo Soldier.*" She eased back in her seat and tried to reform her shattered memory of the night.

She remembered the chase, then nothing, then a drunken waltz through the forest. Kate struggled with the idea that her intense and sudden panic regarding shadow creatures had roused inside her a mental frenzy, which in turn caused her to dash herself against trees and roll over jagged rocks, resulting in the ruined condition of her clothes. She guessed it was possible.

She had heard such defenses utilized in criminal cases, people using wild insanity as a scapegoat for a woodland murder. Katelyn could envision no other scenario to explain her state of disorder, or her blackout. Ghosts, she knew, had not assaulted her in the cool Colorado mountains. That would be insane.

Bob's voice faded and the night host began to yammer. Annoyed, she shut off the radio and drove past Vail in silence, the city's lights glowing and painting the town in the surreal shade of a village on the brink of the new world, untouched and quiet and safe and all sleeping soundly in their beds.

Katelyn's stomach growled. She frowned and swiped her purse off the passenger seat and onto the floor. With her left hand on the steering wheel, she used her right to dig deep behind the seat cushion and retrieve a helping of lint and coins and old peanuts, all of which she dumped into her mouth and swallowed. She did not even care, she was so hungry.

Kate ran out of lint and aged bits of snacks and was on the verge of pulling over to feast on blades of grass and pinecones, whatever bugs she might find in the dirt, when she chanced upon a lonely gas station.

She peeled into the parking lot, stepping on the brakes just in time not to squeal to stop before smashing through the wall. She put the car in park but left the engine running, then fell on the pavement as she tried hurrying into the store. She needed food and she needed it now.

10

Katelyn burst through the door and lashed her head around like a deer that had accidentally broken into that human domain and had no notion of what to do next. Luckily, there was no one in the store at that late hour and the young clerk behind the desk watched what he assumed to be a black girl high on drugs lurch and buck about the shop in confusion. He hit the record button on his phone and filmed Katelyn as she hoofed it down the chip aisle, snatching random bags as she went until her arms were full. She proceeded in a crazed fashion to the checkout.

"Hungry?" the clerk asked, snickering.

Katelyn responded by unloading the chips and her purse on the counter. Her car keys, lip balm, wallet, and everything else spilled out in a clatter of coins and junk. She found her wallet and dug out her only credit card, flicked it at the surprised clerk and tore open a bag of chips. She jammed handfuls between her teeth, crunched and crunched and cut her mouth on the fragments.

She had not yet finished the first bag, crumbs and dust caught in her hair like little orange flies, when she dropped it and opened the second and repeated the act, handful after handful poured over her face and most falling to the floor.

"Hey, I have to clean that up," the clerk said. The humor was finished and now he was annoyed.

Katelyn ignored him. She had opened the third bag, spilling the clutter off the table and shattering her phone screen, and was deep in indulgence. Maddened and starved, desperate to fill a void yet growing inside her, Katelyn tipped the bag to her now bleeding mouth and caught what she could and let the rest fall in a pile.

"Hey!" The clerk said. "You can't do that. I need you to pay for the chips. You can't just throw your credit card at people. You need to enter your pin in the machine."

She glanced briefly at the pimpled gas station clerk, her own face dusted orange, then turned and sprinted with arms outstretched towards the chocolate rack like a crazy woman trying to catch a baby before it splattered on the floor.

She dove into the candy rack and slid to the floor in an avalanche of chocolate bars. Katelyn picked one up, ripped off the wrapper and began to munch. It was the craziest compulsion. Katelyn felt like if she did not eat she would die. She sat slumped against the rack and crammed another chocolate bar into her face.

The clerk exited the safety of his nest and came to stand over the ballistic woman, smeared in chocolate and rolling piggish in her slop.

"I'm going to call the police."

Katelyn kept chewing.

"I mean it. If you don't get up and pay for all this right now, I'm going to call the police and you're going to fucking jail, lady."

Katelyn bit into an unwrapped chocolate bar, chewing plastic and chocolate alike.

"Alright lady, that's it. Hand it over." The clerk reached to try and steal the bar from Katelyn's lunatic jaws, black with blood and black with chocolate. She saw his hand and snarled like a dog.

Some dark instinct. Some bestial tendency from a barbaric age, long since discarded from human proclivity, stirred reborn and powerful in Katelyn. This primitive inclination from man's earliest dawn, when struggle and violence were his only gods, blackened the girl's eyes and clouded her mind with toxic spores that transformed her animal appetite into a sinister compulsion that could not be fought, this ancient thing so symbiotic in nature as to make the girl's blood its home, and also her brain and her bowels and the marrow of her bones. It hijacked her desires and made its own proclamations, and all the while spread its rotten phoenix wings and the girl's spirit fell to ash.

She caught the clerk's hand between her teeth,

the meaty bit of flesh between his thumb and forefinger. There was an awkward moment in which the clerk looked down at her and she stared up at him, just before Katelyn clamped her jaws shut and jerked, came away with blood and wet skin and the clerk shrieked for the gaping red hole in his hand.

He tried to stagger backwards but Katelyn grabbed him before he could away. Feral as she was, a hungry carnivore bloated on sweets, she seized his arm and pulled.

He landed on Katelyn and together they wrestled in her mess of discarded wrappers. The clerk fought meekly and soon succumb. Katelyn was a rabid creature from some dark tribe in a jungle lost to civilization and she battled the clerk with vampiric teeth and nails sharp as talons. She ripped and clawed and sunk her fangs into the boy's cheek and ripped off a hunk of meat. Then she bit his throat out, caught the blood spraying from his arteries in her mouth like it was water from a fountain.

The clerk died. He lay beneath Kate with his skin shredded and his life draining from his twitching body. The profane killer looked down with eyes of round obsidian that showed not remorse nor joy. Katelyn licked her plump lips and smiled, then began to eat.

She flayed skin with teeth and licked at the moist muscles they exposed. She ran her devil's tongue along cuts in the dead boy's face that slowly oozed blood, of which she also drank. She reached into his mouth and pulled his little worm of a tongue out and bit off as much as she could. She did the same to his other soft parts. Katelyn scooped out his eyes and ate them like boiled eggs and even unzipped his pants to gorge on his flaccid penis, sucking the bloodless morsel into her mouth as she had never done with one living and with more satisfaction than if she had.

With the clerk's supple tissue devoured, Katelyn feasted on the sinew of his biceps. She sank her teeth into his muscle in the same wide mouthed manner one might bite into a shiny red apple. She wallowed in the taste of his meat, allowed bubbling crimson to fill her mouth and spill out around her lips.

11

Grant reached the outskirts of Avon, Colorado, at approximately 01:00. He spotted a lone gas station in the dusk of the highway, the indistinct outline of mountains above and beyond it, and decided to fill up one last time and guzzle another coffee before continuing west.

He had started the day eleven hours earlier in Wichita, Kansas, and still had many miles to go before reaching Grand Junction, where he was set to spend a miserable weekend with his estranged family.

It was a far cry from Grant's idea of fun. He would have preferred to spend his weekend catching up on work and fucking his new girlfriend, Sharyl, licking those magnificent nipples of hers until his mouth was numb. However, when his stepfather called and invited him to the first ever family reunion—sure to be overrun with people Grant had never met and would never meet again—he was too chicken-shit to refuse.

As such, Grant left behind Sharyl's pink nipples and drove 750 miles to drink beer and compare his life to the lives of people who may or may not share his blood.

Grant pulled into the gas station. There was only one car in the row of stalls at the front of the building, but he decided for a reason against his knowledge to park opposite it, facing the road. He turned off the engine, grabbed his wallet from the truck's console and got out.

Grant paused beside the box of his truck and breathed in the crisp Colorado air. It was cool and refreshing and he decided to linger a moment longer so he could enjoy the serenity of that calm and noiseless night. He loved the cozy lull of uninhabited space in a land that was alien to him, the empty highway to his rear, the beauty of the stars above and the station's bright windows that made him feel like an astronaut on a barren patch of unexplored planet, his lonely hub an illuminated haven in that lifeless place.

He stretched there in the void, yawned and rattled his weary legs. Looking off toward the station, Grant saw the twisted shadow of some horrible monster rise from behind the parked car and bloat along the exterior wall of the station, peer out at the world with features sunken and claws like curved swords of absent light, then shrink back to where it came like a malicious genie called back into its lamp.

"Huh," he said to himself, "I think I've been awake too long. I'm starting to see things."

Grant gave his head a shake and started across the parking lot. He eyed the wall suspiciously, anticipating the demonic shade to rise once more. He reached the door and moved to enter, had his hand on the handle and was a second away from stumbling upon something heinous, when he was startled by the vague shape of a woman slumped against the bumper of what he assumed to be her car.

She looked to have been shot. It was hard to tell in the darkness, but she was slouched and limp as if dead; legs spread, arms languid on the cement, head drooped and hair dangling.

"Hey," Grant said, letting go of the door and walking over to her, "are you alright?"

She moved a bit. Her arms jerked and one leg twitched.

"Do you want me to call 911? Do you need an ambulance?"

She groaned, mumbled something inaudible.

Grant stepped over Katelyn's leg and knelt to get a better look at her. "What? Are you trying to say something?"

She struggled to raise her head. It was as though the weight of her brain and skull were too much for her neck. Then she coughed blood in Grant's face.

He fell back against the gas station wall and shouted some profanity, wiping his eyes with his sleeve. "What the hell is wrong with you?"

She did not look at him. Her eyes were closed and her face sagged over the ground. She looked sick. Katelyn lurched forward and started to gag.

Grant looked on in horror as Katelyn vomited between her legs. An unthinkable mass of black sludge poured from Katelyn's mouth and splattered on the concrete, so much dark sewer water spewing from her face that within seconds there was a small pool of runny tar on the ground and still she expelled more.

"Fuck," Grant said in disbelief.

Katelyn raised her head and rested the back of her skull against the car's headlight, current spilling over her bottom lip in a dark sheet and soaking her ripped blouse and exposed bra. The remnants of Katelyn's meal lay in a disgusting pile at her crotch like a heap of moist black moss pulled from the ground, none of it quite digested and some of it solid.

"What have you taken?" Grant asked.

She said nothing.

"I need you to tell me. It's important. I'm going

to call an ambulance now and they're going to need to know what made you sick."

Katelyn said, "No."

"What do you mean no?"

"No."

She grabbed Grant by his collar, and it was then when she opened her eyes and he saw them to be as black as the gunk she had purged. He also saw her teeth. They were stained red, and in contrast to the oily goo smeared over her face were very bright.

Grant tried to pull away, but she forced him close and regurgitated ebony slime into his mouth and all over his face in a messy geyser. She let go of Grant and he fell in a spastic fit while Katelyn relaxed against the car with residue bubbling at her mouth.

Grant clawed at his face and kicked the air. "Get it off!" The sentient goo crept down his throat and he coughed and gagged. "Get it off!" It spread throughout his body like the virus it was, filtering into every system and entering each network of vein and nerve and sticking to his muscles. It washed over his face, into his ears and up his nose. It seeped into the corners of his eyes and set them to burning. Grant had never felt such pain.

12

They left the gas station in Grant's truck. Katelyn sat in the passenger seat and together they drove along the interstate in grim silence.

After a while Katelyn said, "My mom's dying. She's in Sacramento."

"Sorry to hear that."

"I don't really care."

"I don't really care either. I'm hungry."

"I'm hungry too."

They drove on through the night, stopping once to hunker around a smear of roadkill and fight the buzzards for its rancid meat and festering innards. They stopped once more before daybreak to wash the deer's blood and grossness off themselves in a creek beside the road. Then they continued west until the sun threatened to rise.

They slept through the day in a dirty motel with the shades drawn. They slept in the same bed without blankets and fully clothed. When the daylight died, Katelyn and Grant drove west in search of food.

OTAKTAY, KILLS MANY

THOU WRATH
SHALL SCORCH
THE PLANES OF
EARTH

J. Cortex

1

He sat a grim council with the shadows, that lone man
in the depths of nowhere.

The obscurities lingered at the fringe of light
cast quivering over sand and stone by fires he had built
around him, five pits dug in the desert floor and filled
with brush and set to burning to stave away the night.
These unnatural beings danced and frolicked to a deaf
beat. Their swaying forms were lies; elongated, ghostly,
always in flux. Sparks were belched from the fiery pits
and carried along the wind to swirl about these
silhouettes and they appeared to be a league of cinder-
born jesters from some sordid court in the city of Dis.
The little orange flakes of residual inferno were the
same as those propagated in that palace of brimstone,
and they flocked to the opaque harlequins as if they
held sprinklers in their dim hands and twirled them in
a ritualistic performance there in the blackness, trying
to coax the man from his shelter.

The outcast watched without humor. His legs
were crossed and he wore a loincloth to conceal his
manhood. Otherwise, he was naked, pecks firm, back
straight, hands cupped in his lap like a monk deep in
meditation. His tawny skin was filthy with sand and
with dirt, though his long hair was glossy and free down
his back, reflective in the fire light.

With chestnut eyes, Otaktay observed the
taunting shadows, yet he himself was undaunted by
their grotesque waltz and he was vigilant in his

watching, for he hated those vile fiends and knew well their nature. Despite all their evil, Otaktay knew they dare not enter the ring of light—the wall of fire conjured by a red-skinned outcast who sat rigid and unafraid within his armor of incandescence.

Soon, he would stoke the fires for the last time that night. He would distribute heaps of big sagebrush and kindling and ensure the vigor of each blaze before laying on the rocky ground and looking at the stars. He would sleep. He would sleep and the flames would dance the same free dance of the nightfall stalkers. Come morning, the cursed haunts would be gone, his pyres reduced to ash and dead embers. He would burry the holes and move on.

2

He traveled the sagebrush sea of Southern Idaho beneath a blazing sun and without shoes. The daytime heat was intense in that wasteland and sweat trickled down his brow as he kept a steady pace. Luckily for Otaktay, his red skin was adapted to such an arid climate, and so he persevered without clothes or footwear, for his feet were hooves that tread across the land of his ancestors and he traversed the open wilderness of wind and sand and rock and not a scrap of foliage above his waist unscathed. He did not stumble, nor trip, nor tire. He never once lost his way. He never muttered a complaint.

The Indian understood the rugged terrain of Owyhee County, a wide berth of land that encompassed much of Northern Nevada and Southern Idaho. It was a large region devoid of human existence, other than a few natives who lived in the Duck Valley Indian Reserve, perhaps 1,000 in total and almost all in the city of Owyhee, which lay just under the borderline.

As a boy raised in that isolated place, Otaktay

learned of his ancient heritage, of the land, and of the beasts who roamed it.

Tribal elders and the clan shaman bestowed upon Otaktay an abundance of knowledge, which they themselves had inherited from the generation before them. Those wise old men with their wrinkled skin and archaic costumes summoned the boy into tepees made of tanned hide and painted with rings of suns and designs of stallions, and there, before a small fire, they taught him things. They taught him that power (puha) resided in every natural object, such as the sun, moon, thunder, clouds, stars, and wind; and they explained to him that any man could harness those energies to assist him in hunting and in battle, and in fathering a child.

Otaktay was also educated on the importance of all living creatures and how none held greater position than the other and how all shared the Earth's bounty. He was schooled in the unique characteristics of plants and animals, how to utilize them without waste, what role the falcon and the beetle and the mountain played in the world, and how none could survive without the other.

Perhaps his favorite teachings were of myth. With the old men's faces washed in firelight and their naked chests red as clay, the tent black but for the small area they sat, Otaktay listened to lore and legend and stories of gods.

He heard of Ena, the wolf and creator god. Ena's brother, the coyote, who was a trickster spirit and always getting into trouble. The Nimerigar, a violent race of tiny folk who killed and ate men for sport. Water babies, awful creatures who inhabited springs and ponds. They killed babes and took their place as changelings, and sometimes mimicked the sound of a crying infant to lure men to watery graves.

There were other folktales. Fables of Thunder Birds and of the Stone Mother, Coyote's trip to the Sun, a woman's escape from a cannibal monster. But the narrative that roused the most dread in Otaktay's young heart was the story of a man from pioneer days. A deranged lunatic seduced and scorned by the Skudakumooch, his children murdered and devoured, his township destroyed by the witch's evil.

Other lessons included the history of the Northern Paiute, from the peaceful clans in the 1700s to the introduction of the white man in 1820, the Pyramid Lake War of 1860 and the Bannock war of 1878, the gradual loss of culture and tradition, the rise of the ghost dance.

And expectedly, Otaktay learned how to hunt and fish, how to skin and cook and forage and heal, create fire and shelter and to live off the land, herd cattle and mount a horse.

It was as if Otaktay had been conditioned to be a prominent member of the Northern Paiute tribe from the day of his birth, though no one knew why. He was hated amongst his peers, his family, and even those who taught him.

None of that mattered now. He was cast out, shunned, never again welcome in his homeland.

3

Things learned can not be unlearned, much in the same way a thing seen can not be unseen, even if eyes are burned or removed entirely. Otaktay still knew the names of the indigenous wildlife. He knew the subtle differences between gray rabbitbrush and green rabbitbrush, those small shrubs that dotted the landscape and were the benefactors of much desert life. He knew that the netleaf hackberry tree was the tallest plant to grow on the foothills. It could live for

200 years, though in the barren drawl he now roamed there were little of these scraggly plants. He was also well acquainted with the aase's onion and its purple flowers, the yellow arrowleaf balsamroot that he could see sprouting in the sandy soil of the lowlands through which he traveled.

No, expulsion could not erase his familiarity with the scabrous realm he had been discarded in and left to die. Every flower that rose from a patch of stones or a mud-filled gully like a singular thing of beauty in an ugly province, he knew its name and its properties. He could make blue dye from the bastard toadflex with nothing but clay and time. He knew that if he held a flame to a patch of cheatgrass, the flame would feed and spread and prosper and ravage whole acres until the ground was a vast inferno and when it ceased to burn the soil would be black and things that had lived would be dead.

4

He meandered west through plains of dingy grass and gnarled brush and sometimes nothing but rock. He stepped over holes in the ground where serpents lay coiled tight as springs with fangs and tails that rattled. There were other pits in the earth; gopher burrows tucked within tangles of foliage and thin grottos in the rugged earth where small dragons and their kin slept at night, and in the day crept to flat rocks to bask in the sun and flick their tongues and flare their beards. Otaktay's foot fell near one of these golden eyed reptiles and it quickly sprinted inside a complex of tiny stones, like the collapsed temple of an advanced race of insects, and was gone. Birds with huge wings made slow circles around the plate sun. They seemed curious Otaktay's state of life.

He had with him an axe. He carried it in his

right hand as though he marched with the intent of some holy retribution. A brown satchel was tied about his waist and it contained a few items. He had no food, no water. His stomach grumbled with each step and each time he tried to swallow his mouth proved too parched. He stopped a moment, looked up at the blazing sun perched at its zenith, looked west, and continued on.

In the distance rose blanched hills that looked to be sand dunes. In the brightness they were white, but he knew them to be speckled with gray rocks and wheatgrass and desert flowers, endless sagebrush. After a while he crested one of these mounds and surveyed the landscape, hand to brow.

Otaktay could see for miles. Far to the west was an evident split in the Earth, but from such a distance it looked miniscule, maybe even a trick. The heat that rose off the surface of the desert made aspects blurry and inconsistent. He saw the great basin of Southern Idaho. It was calm and quiet. Hills and rock formations dotted the panorama but most was flat. Centuries ago, there would have been groups of buffalo, deer, and other migrating beasts, but the new world orphans had arrived and shot every animal with their rifles in such pitiless number that the country was now vacant and only those small critters not worth their hide or meat lived and they hid.

That night he dug five pits in a shallow valley and filled them with sticks and twigs and grass and roots. He ignited them as night began to fall and when all five crackled he took his place in their core.

He sat cross legged and naked, save for his loincloth, and he watched shadows materialize and one by one line the hill before him like a platoon of shaded archers in formation. He watched that flank of midnight bowmen with apathy, and they in turn glared at him. That night none of them moved. They appeared to be an afterimage scarred on the flesh of darkness that was draped over the land, ghosts of soldiers who had once set ambush there on that hill in a time since forgotten.

He lay down amidst flames. Five towers of smoke rose from the burning pyres and they swirled overhead and merged to form a white nebula that obscured the stars. He slept. Come morning, the sentinels of animated blackness were gone and the fires smoldered and were gray and a few coals were still warm. Otaktay buried them along with his waste and continued west.

5

The exile could have fled east. After he had wrestled free of the ropes that bound him and stood with the desert sand between his toes and looked about at the destitute region in which he had been so cruelly abandoned and left to die, he could have gone east. Twin falls or the highway would have been a faster walk. From there, he could have hitchhiked. To where, he could not have said. What to do when he arrived, well, he would not have known that either.

The Indian had no money, no clothes, no material for trade except his flesh. He would have been a vagabond in a civilization that, regardless of its proximity, was infinitely alien to him. The white men's lives of motors and cable and credit and fashion were known to Otaktay in the same way a man might comprehend the rocks on Pluto; aware of their existence and that they are rocks, but confounded by their properties, applications, colors, textures.

The only thing that made sense in his mind was to roam west to Bruneau Canyon. He figured to establish a primitive homestead there beside the river and be sheltered by the canyon walls. Then, in his solitude, Otaktay would discover a way to combat the scourge of shadows that pursued him, and thus, claim retribution for his slain kin.

The details of this plan were obscure even to him. Yet he could imagine no place else to go.

6

By dusk of the follow day he was drained. Thirst and hunger had taken their toll on Otaktay and he staggered stupid and weak across the prairie. He stubbed his toes on rocks and tripped over roots camouflaged against the pastel floor like snares set by nature. And though the canyon remained a day's walk, he was stubborn as a mule and strayed too far in the sun's fleeting light without consideration for the onset of darkness. By the time he stopped to make camp, a grizzly shade had encompassed the land.

He used the flat side of his axe to break apart the Earth's hard outer shell and reveal the loose soil beneath. Then he used his hands to hollow out bowl shaped craters that could have been shallow graves for children This was the hardest labor of the evening and when he was done all five holes his hands were brown with muck and it was caked under his fingernails and his knees were sore. He laid a bed of dry grass in each pit as though they were indeed graves and the perished young needed soft mattresses to lay upon, then he filled them with shrubs and sticks and any hard wood he could find.

He collected extra material and amassed it in the center of the dugouts where he would sleep. He gathered all the large stones he could find and made pathetic walls around his excavations. He moved with slow, methodical ease from pit to pit. The sun sank below the horizon. The sky blackened.

The native was hunkered with a flint in hand.

He shot sparks at kindling and soon the first blaze was lit and it emitted a deep red aura in the darkness but shone little light.

He stood and his body looked powerful in the dimness of the fire. He peered into the growing flames and they reflected in his brown eyes and the look on his face was stern. Otaktay's sable hair hung to one side, the muscles of his back lean and his pecks carved. He had the aspect of a tribal warrior on some fateful quest, alone in the world and alone on that cold desert plain.

He turned to ignite the next pyre and a shade stood blocking his path. It simply loomed there as if by invitation and though it had no face it seemed to leer. Otaktay eyed the manifest of gloom defiantly for a moment, then withdrew and hunkered next to the campfire.

They settled into a tense stand off. The human was cast in the fire's red aura and the shadow threatened to be a hallucination by the way it jittered.

He scooped up a handful of sand. "Be gone with you." And tossed the sand at the shadow as if the beige mist would dissolve it. The phantom remained, taunting, shuddering, quivering, and the sand fell slowly through its spectral blackness like gravity held no rule there in its bowels.

Otaktay frowned. He pulled a flaming stick from the fire. "Be gone." And threw it. His torch disintegrated the shadow's dark quiddity on impact and fell extinguished to the ground.

He snatched a new one from the crackling brush and quickly moved from pit to pit until all were aflame and he was safe in their collective glow for another night.

A horde of umbra loitered in the twilight and

watched Otaktay as he slept. Their oily compositions were vivid on the outskirts of yellow light and they were patient in their lingering. They waited all through the midnight shroud and encroached inch by inch as the flames dwindled and only when dawn banished them back to Hell did they retreat.

7

Otaktay reached Bruneau Canyon an hour before nightfall.

He stood on the fringe of a sheer drop some 350 meters deep, nudged a stone off the edge and watched it skitter down the canyon wall and trigger a small avalanche, debris cascading downwards and coming to rest somewhere at the bottom in a puff of dust.

He stepped back and looked across the gorge. It was a massive split in the Earth. It divided the land as far as his eye could see. He gazed north, and the way the fissure was formed made him think of how a block of timber fractures when struck by a woodsman's axe, a behemoth cracking open the globe with a swing of his giant hammer.

He inspected the western interior of that schism. Its makeup was beige and red and brown and smooth in some places where in others it was uneven. There appeared to be walkways that ran its length like old mining trails, but they led to nothing. A black line of sediment marked the place where eons ago the planet had shifted and perhaps there was a flood. Perhaps an extinction event, or maybe a terrible fire that had burnt the Earth's crust and made it black. He wondered if millions of years ago there was a volcano that had erupted and boiling red magma flowed through the chasm, and if the ash and the heat from that river of fire had scorched the land he now stood on and that was why it was dry and infertile and almost nothing lived. He wondered but he did not know.

Otaktay peered over the edge one more time at the basin. He saw the blue water of the serpentine river that weaved through the lightning shaped wound in mother nature's flesh, and he saw the flanks of lush greenery on either side and looked on with longing. There were trees down there. Not many, but enough. There was green grass and healthy plants and water to drink. There was sanctuary.

He glanced over his shoulder and immediately looked away, for the sun was a raging ball of fire at the brink of existence and the sky was flamboyant pink, the environment below glittering like gold.

The man frowned. It would not be long before the shadows came out to play and to tease. He would have to make camp there on the precipice, lest he risk another confrontation with a ghoul of night.

Otaktay spotted an area to the south where the bluff slanted. It looked to be an incline of rock beaten by decades of wind, a kind of ramp formed from erosion, the shattered section of a great wall where men could scurry up over the rubble. Beneath that was a barrier of red stone and jagged pillars of rock like massive stalagmites all fused together. Below the solid mass was another slant of loose sediment. Come morning, Otaktay figured he could slide down the embankment, navigate a route through the blockade of earth, and reach safety in the valley below.

Wood was scarce so near the gap and he had to wander to find it. He hacked apart knee-high trees with branches of thistle that were entwined chaotically. He had to drag these to the chasm's edge where he made a pile. It took a long time, but eventually he was well stocked with sagebrush and sticks.

He dug his ditches. He filled them. The sky

turned magenta and he paused his work to watch the sun flare on the horizon, shrink and then bloom yellow like the afterglow of an apocalyptic explosion in a far away city.

The fires were lit soon after. They roared and sparks careened into the air and each pit radiated dark red and the flames were quite yellow and the world outside that dome of incandescence was very black.

8

Otaktay had come across a rattlesnake earlier in the day, hiding amongst some rocks. He had found a flimsy branch that worked to hold down the serpent's neck, and with a stone he had bashed in its head, then coiled it up like one would a belt and stuffed it into his satchel. Now, with an audience of faceless apparitions, he peeled off its skin and cooked its meat over one of the fires.

It was Otaktay's first meal since his ostracism and it filled his empty stomach in a way most sublime. He chewed small pieces without much hurry and as he ate, the wind picked up. By the time he had consumed the whole snake and sat cross legged and satisfied, harsh gusts were causing his fires to panic and writhe uncontrollably, the smoke to blow every which way.

The shadows were just as susceptible to this malign force of nature. They remained grounded but their murky bodies fluttered like sheets on a line. Some were even fueled by the belligerent element and they grew large enough in size to have squashed Otaktay under their giant black feet if they were not cowards in the light. Others puffed like fat men with large guts and some blew sideways so their anatomies were quite obtuse, so the Indian could not tell arms from legs. They became a legion of malformed balloons and they celebrated their gigantism there on the canyon ridge with hails to the wind, yet those hails may just have been the wind itself.

Otaktay lay down with a full stomach and the flames so close to his person they burned his skin, even when he curled in the center.

He could not sleep. Several hours past with him curled in a ball in the dirt and the flames lashing out at him. Still he could not sleep.

Otaktay's insomnia was not caused by the freak show around him, the imps with warped structures that shrank and bloated like shadows of monsters in some ridiculous cartoon. No, he was restless because his sister haunted him when he closed his eyes. She stared at him in that void of darkness and her face was more terrifying than any hell spawn.

ONIDA, THE ONE SEARCHED FOR

Sister, the dying light of my heart

1

She gave birth on a cold night in October, inside a hut where a fire raged and the air was humid.

She squatted naked above a bed of leaves laid out for the newborn to fall upon. She was young and beautiful, glistening with sweat. Her long hair was drenched and hung down her back and collected on the floor. As her contractions came and went, her face strained and relaxed and blushed a dozen shades of red. Her milk engorged breasts rested on her swollen belly, which was a pale brown egg in the yellow radiance of the fire that washed over her and the midwife, that old crone reciting some archaic hymn meant to coax the babe from the womb.

They were but two inside the sweltering hut and they labored for many hours. The midwife's crazed chant was perpetual and grew in fervor, became something akin to a shaman's mad attempt at resurrection and she sometimes danced in a way that seemed insane.

The baby's head appeared and cries resonated inside the hut. Its shoulders stretched the woman's vagina and dark liquid dribbled onto the leaves. She pushed and pushed and soon it entered the world, squalling and falling, still tethered to its mother, and landed on the leafy bed. The child writhed there, a red grub all sticky and shrill in its afterbirth.

The midwife fixed her old eyes on the baby and declared it a girl. She grabbed hold of the umbilical cord like it was a wild snake and cut it with a dagger appropriated for such a ritual. She held up the wailing infant with both hands in an odd display of victory for the mother to see, because she had collapsed of exhaustion.

The father would look at his baby girl and declare her the most adorable child in the world, then destine her to grow into the most beautiful of women. He named her Onida. In the tongue of their people it meant, 'The One Searched For.'

She was the first born.

2

His entrance into the world was unfortunate and violent. He arrived upon a wave of blood, amidst a sea of gore. His young mother lay stark on the ground with her eyes lifeless to the ceiling and her face twisted in a concluding expression of agony. Her stomach was unnaturally deflated and her breasts sagged and her legs were arched upwards as though contrary to death she would still give life, her vagina gaped and blood flowing from it like a drainpipe discharging red sewage, her son squirming beneath the deluge and so burdened in her essence that he appeared a crimson cherub dumped in a cradle of dark vomit.

The midwife sneered down at the crying boy, splashing there in the puddle of slop. She bent and severed his cord without care. She lifted him by one leg and dangled him before her and she slapped the boy and scolded him for the brutal way in which he came to be. She carried him that way, far from her body like a rank corpse, to the fire at the core of the hut, where she held him above the flames.

"You are a stealer of life," she said, the flames themselves enraged by his presence. "You are a demon—an evil spirit incarnated inside the body of an infant. You leeched the energy of an innocent woman to be manifested in human form and for that I should drop you into the flames and watch you reduced to ash and bone."

The threat excited the fire and its incandescence flared and the whole hut bloomed red.

"But I won't. I will permit you life, for it is not my place to slay infants, evil or otherwise. Yet hear me now, foul incubus: you *are* cursed, and you *will* live a solemn life without the love of any woman, and in your heart will grow a great shame. Your existence will end in more blood than it began, for that is your fate and I deem it so."

Her hand where she held him burned and steam hissed from the baby's moist scalp and he cried and cried, there in the hut where his sister was born and his mother died.

His father agreed with the midwife and called his son a killer. He received him with hate and scorn and accepted him only because of a father's duty. He named him Otaktay, which in the tongue of their people meant, 'Kills Many.'

He was the second born.

3

Onida and her brother grew up in the town of Owyhee, in a trailer with their father.

He was a drunk. He collected money from the government and refused to work. His days were spent at home in front of the television, his evenings at the only pub in town where he would drink and sleep where he fell. He loved his daughter. He hated his son. He blamed Otaktay for the loss of his wife.

Onida and Otaktay went to the same small school, in which all the other students were of the Northern Paiute. She did well and so did he. She made friends and he did not. She grew to be the stunning beauty her father had fated, and even Otaktay grew to be a strong, attractive teenager.

Though for all his good looks, Otaktay was

odd and out of place. In such a close-knit community, there was no room for a boy with a different constitution than the others, and so he was ignored.

Yet for some unknown reason, the elders—for indeed they still feigned their old traditions—took it upon themselves to teach the dejected youngster all they knew.

They showed him favor but no kindness. They schooled him and nothing more. When his lessons were complete, they shunned him as if they had taught him by accident and regretted the whole affair. They treated him with the same contempt his peers did.

Onida had quite the opposite adolescence. She was adored by everyone: boys, teachers, friends, strangers. She was smart and gorgeous and exalted among the residents of Owyhee. She was also the only person who showed Otaktay any love, as he was her brother and she would always love him.

A week before Onida graduated their father died of kidney failure. She was heartbroken and became sick with grief, and at his funeral she cried. Otaktay held his composure at that morose event and mourned candidly as was expected of him, but under that facade there was no sadness.

Onida married soon after and she left their family home to live with her new husband, Naheen. Otaktay finished school two years later without ever knowing the touch of a woman. Rather than stay in the home of his father, where memories of his depressing childhood were evident in every corner of that rundown place, he moved to the outskirts of town and erected a large tepee there, where he lived on a dusty patch of land in solitude.

Years went by.

Onida's husband died. He was out riding his favorite horse and the animal tripped in a rut and fell and crushed Naheen under its immense weight. His ribs snapped and pierced his lungs and they filled with blood and he choked and died there on the plains of northern Nevada. They found him two days later, ugly, rotted, picked apart by coyotes and vultures.

In the wake of tragedy, Onida sought comfort with her brother. She packed some things and he welcomed her into his modest home. He set up a cot for her beside his and they resided there for several months and it was indeed the happiest time of the man's life.

Growing up neglected and despised, being accused of murdering his mother, had transformed Otaktay into—not a jaded man, but one of immense loneliness, subject to severe bouts of depression, fatigue, self-pity, and general sadness. He spoke little and only to his sister, and so when she came to live with him, despite the calamitous reason for her refuge, it warmed Otaktay's heart in a benign way and spread a smile across his unkissed lips.

4

Onida was out late on a Tuesday in May. She had gone to the river to bathe in the moonlight and had not yet returned and it was near midnight. Otaktay had advised her against it, but Onida never did believe in her brother's superstitious nonsense and she went anyway.

He was hunkered by the fire, awaiting her return with an ugly feeling in his gut. He had just placed a kettle on a metal grate over the flames and decided that when it whistled, he would mount a search. Until then, he stared through the slots of burning wood at the basin of ash and ember and his thoughts were as dead as the cinders that flaked apart there.

Carnivores

Onida pulled aside the flap and entered the tepee. Smoke funneled out through the hole in the roof and below that was her brother, obscure behind the pyre's main flame.

She lingered inside the door. Her posture was slack, her shadow thrown against the wall in a thin and ominous, vampiric sort of way, how it breathed and crept. There were crude paintings of ravens near the entrance, their wings spread and their heads tilted skyward. They seemed agitated by Onida's shadow and even the fire grew unnerved. Flames sputtered and sparks flew, and Otaktay looked up to see his sister loitering strangely near the door.

He stood, and at first noticed nothing awry. He saw his beautiful sister, her hair in two long braids from neck to waist, tied near their bottoms with white bands. She wore a casual long dress, beige and opulent in dizzy patterns of yellow, blue, red.

Then Otaktay realized her shoes were missing. Her bare feet were filthy and her flower necklace was gone, her neck red where it had been as though someone had strangled her with wire. A wound on the top of her skull, where her hair parted, was moist and dark. Her eyes were black.

"Sister, what happened to you at the river this night?"

She gave no reply, stepped languidly to the fire with her head tilted and stared spellbound into its flames.

"Sister, I asked you what happened. How did you injure yourself? What madness has possessed you?"

Onida did look mad. Her lips were spread in a devilish grin and her blackened eyes were huge and reflected the flames she gawked at.

The kettle whistled and steam exploded from

its spout. Onida placed her hands out before her, as if to warm them, then smiled wider as she reached into the fire and grabbed the kettle by its handle.

Otaktay heard flesh sizzle and smelled the tangy odor of singed human. Onida took the piping hot ketal from the fire, gave it a brief look, and tossed it at him.

Otaktay jumped out of the way and the container flew by, boiling water spiraling out of it. "Sister, stop this insanity. Whatever's taken you, fight it!"

She looked at him and smiled but made no sound. She then moved around the fire towards him and he stepped away and they began a slow dance around the pit. She walked right and he walked left, and always Otaktay kept the blaze between them.

"End this." His voice fraught with desperation. "Fight the darkness I see in your eyes. Force it out. You are too strong to be corrupted by evil!"

She did not hear his words. She stopped walking and so did he and he looked pathetic and on the verge of tears, and Onida watched his mouth move but all the things he said about maleficent spirits in the night and the possession of bodies and his study on the origin of a curse that spawned them were lost in the crackle of the fire and the pounding of her heart.

He stopped talking and they stared quietly at one another. Onida looked extraterrestrial to him, her face consumed by giant black eyes that never blinked and might have held the vastitude of the universe within them.

Onida saw a victim. She saw a weak thing in her infinite vision and it offended her. She wanted to hurt it, to kill it. The longer she stared, the angrier she became. Her smile faded and her visage soured into a nasty grimace and she growled like a beast and leapt over the fire, grappled with Otaktay and they spun and fell to the ground.

She clawed and hissed, foamed at the mouth and beat on Otaktay's face, but Onida's possession gave her no supernatural strength and her brother soon mounted her.

She was berserk, flailing and yowling. Otaktay became lost in his own mania. A savage instinct reddened his sight and somewhere in the brawl he reached for his axe and he buried it in his sister's face.

Blood seeped from where metal fused with flesh and Onida, for a moment, did not seem dead at all, merely inconvenienced by the axe stuck crosswise in her head.

The brown returned to her eyes and little black tadpoles swam in the crimson that wept down her cheeks. Otaktay was stunned and he stood above her, watching black slime filter from her blood and slither towards him with sentient resolve.

He backed away and the sludge gave chase like an alien plasma discharged from a meteor and in dire need of a host. Adrenaline still pumped inside him and he reached with both arms into the fire and pulled burning pieces of timber toward him and the whole thing spilled over. In the chaos, a flaming log rolled onto the swarm of darkness and it fizzled and shrank like a singed slug.

His tepee was on fire. Flames inched up the hide walls and the whole place was filling with ash and smoke. Frantic, Otaktay snatched his sister by the leg and dragged her from the wreckage with the tool still bored in her head and it jostled as he hauled her corpse to the dirt outside.

He crouched and watched his patchwork house be consumed, the ravens he had painted burn and crumble to dust. He sat until his home was little more than a bonfire on an empty prairie and he sat with the cold remains of his sister beside him and eventually he rose and went for help.

5

He led a mob to the scene of devastation and when they saw the axe buried in Onida's head they raged and someone pushed Otaktay to the ground. He landed beside the grotesque carcass of his sister and would have shrieked if not for a foot swiftly kicking him in the gut. Another followed. The people spat on him, called him a murderer and an abomination.

They bound him with rope and all the while he pleaded and preached of dark spirits, but no one cared. They told Otaktay he was insane, unwell, and a liar, and as dawn approached they banished him and sentenced him to a slow death in the wild.

He was slung carelessly over the back of a horse and the rider rode for one day and one night and on the second morning he dumped Otaktay in a patch of desert bare and brown to every extent.

He writhed constricted in the dirt like some abandoned masochist and the rider looked down with disgust. He threw Otaktay his axe, stained in the blood of his kin, and rode off.

Leaving the weapon had not been a gift or a kindness, but rather a reminder to drive Otaktay mad with guilt. It was not uncommon for a man to lose his mind when forlorn in the desolate waste.

SICK INDULGENCES

Incorruptible corruption

J. Cortex

HORACE & MARY

1

Horace knew something was wrong. The old bull
could feel it. He drove into Yakima County wondering
why they had left Mary's house after sunset, not after
sunrise. It did not make a ton of sense. Horace never
did have the best night vision. And that was another
thing. His glasses were gone but he could see just fine.
In fact, Horace could see better than he had in years.
Felt better, too. Horace felt strong, in his prime again.
He felt like a young bull as he coasted down the
highway, Mary's hot breath in his ear.

"You want me to do it again, love?"

This was also new, this sexual fever. Horace
had lost his libido a few years ago, or at least the will to
use it. Now sex was all he could think about. His body
warmed and he grew ravenous at the thought.

"Yes, Mary. Please do it again."

Mary got her knees up on the seat and bent
into Horace's crotch, unclasped his belt once more
and pulled out his dick. It was still hard from last time,
from an hour ago when Horace had blasted a cold
splurge of inky-black semen into Mary's mouth.

She, like him, was eager for more. She was
eager to milk it out of him. Mary sucked Horace off
from the passenger seat, slurping and licking and
fondling his balls.

It quieted the need he had for it. Horace eased
back with one hand on the wheel and watched the

bright lights of Yakima come into view. Those lights unnerved him for a reason he could not understand. He turned left onto Highway 12 and drove on through the dark, away from the lights.

Horace's memory was fogged. There were blank patches where there should have been hours. He reckoned he had smacked his head pretty hard on the steering wheel last night, because a lot of the time after was a blur. And even now, as Horace squeezed the steering wheel with both hands and spasmed a load of cum into Mary's throat, he felt to be missing something. It was as if he could not connect the dots, could not keep his thoughts in order, could not rectify what was wrong.

Mary sat up and wiped her mouth. "Mm. Thanks for that, darling."

"There's more where that came from," Horace said, the vile urge already rebuilding. Those words were not his; they never had been. He was so lost in this new abyss of sexual endeavor that he muttered dirtiness like a pervert with Tourette syndrome. "I'll fill you with cum, you little fucking bitch."

Mary smiled greedily. She wanted more. A lot more. She was infected by lust, gyrating impatiently in her seat as they drove on through the dark Wednesday night in search of primal places.

2

Horace still had a mind to explore America's backroads, to camp out and build fires and be one with the wilderness. He supposed Mary did too, since she was there with him. He could not recall asking her to come. She had packed a bag and got in the truck. They were partners now, two giddy old folks discovering what it was like to be horny teenagers again. Neither realized the disease gestating in their blood.

They drove past the settlements of Gleed, Eschbach, and Naches, then west over the Naches River bridge. They were very handsy, groping each other and giggling while the blacktop stretched flat and slick beyond the headlights. They drove on beside the Tieton River and entered Wenatchee National Forest.

Horace said, "Quiet country out here, eh Mary? Yeah, I figure a man could live out here in these wilds. Susan would have loved it here."

"Ay. Marcus too."

To their right were small mountains sparse with trees, the woods dark and thick with spruce to their left. All along the roadside were the shadows of men like midnight hitchhikers trying to hitch a ride back to Hell.

They came upon a sign: *Windy Point Campground.*

Horace said, "What do you think, Mary? Windy Point Campground. Should we check it out?"

"It's low season," she said. "There shouldn't be many people camping. It'll be just the two of us. Just the two love birds and no one to hear our song. I'd say we take a gander."

Horace liked the sound of that, him and Mary alone and no one to hear her scream. He sped up the road until the turnoff for the campground, veered left and jostled down the gravel drive until they reached the grounds.

He did a circuit of the place and it looked deserted. The truck's high-beams washed over plots of empty land, unused picnic tables, and vacant stalls where motorhomes would be abundant come high season. Horace saw trails leading off into the forest that made him contemplate a midnight hike, fucking Mary in a cluster of prickle bushes, and he saw the long dead remnants of campfires, shards of glass turned black and jaded in the ashes.

"As good a place as any," Horace said. He was anxious to get unpacked, set up the tent and crawl inside with Mary and do terrible things to her until dawn. The lust he had was unquenchable. It had arisen from nowhere to poison his mind and now Horace's thoughts were submerged beneath a sea of black, gooey hunger. He could barely hear himself think. He listened instead to the instinctual craving he had for soft, warm flesh.

"Wait." Mary pointed out the windshield, at a white sedan parked on some grass and a green tent erected beside it, a pair of young campers in flannel sitting by a fire and drinking beer. "We're not the only love birds in the nest."

"Looks that way, Mary. Looks that way."

Horace stopped the truck in front of the kids' campsite, headlights blinding the poor campers. They shielded their eyes and squinted at the unexpected glare of light, this harbinger of unknown danger in such an isolated region.

"They look lonely," Mary said. "Lonely and alone and all by their lonesome. We should say hello."

Horace parked two lots up from the lovers. He and Mary exited the truck and unloaded their supplies under the glow of the headlamps. Neither had constructed a tent in decades, and so they laughed and teased as they fought with the collapsible poles, through trial and error finally establishing the thing in a proper dome shape. Mary dragged their bedding inside and made the interior nice and cozy while Horace built a fire.

3

Horace and Mary stood away from their fire, not quite liking the light of it.

"It's too bright," Horace said. "I can feel the fire boiling my blood."

Mary nodded. She could feel it too, the radiance of the fire agitating whatever darkness flowed through her bloodstream.

It seemed asinine to Horace that he should suddenly have an irrational fear of flames. Yet he did. They unnerved him on an intrinsic level. He stared into the fire, hypnotized by its hellish nature, feeling his flesh prickle and sting.

Mary was getting antsy. "We should say hello to the youngsters. They look lonely."

"What about us?" Horace was still eager to get his rocks off. The need was killing him. It was an itch on the inside of his skin that he could not scratch.

"What if they want to join us?" Mary said.

Now that was an idea. Horace's murky eyes opened wide and a hot sensation swirled in his belly. They had looked young, that couple, perhaps in their twenties. Horace began to imagine how soft and firm they must be, how tight and fresh. He wiped a spot of drool from his chin and said, "Yes, we should ask them."

Horace and Mary walked across the two empty lots and came upon the campers and their fire.

"Hello," Horace said in his most neighborly voice. "Sorry to disturb you. My friend was saying how lonely you look over here by yourselves. She reckoned we should come say hi."

The couple exchanged a confused glance, caught off-guard by the smiley old people. Horace and Mary looked sinister on the other side of the campfire, a touch malign with their friendly grins huge in the firelight.

"Thanks for the concern," the boy said, "but

we're not lonely, man. We're camping together. We didn't think anyone else would be here."

"Us neither," Mary said. "But funny, isn't it, how God puts us all in the same place? What are your names, darlings?"

"I'm Julian. This is my girlfriend, Wendi."

Wendi gave them an awkward wave, but she was not impressed by Horace and Mary's intrusion. She was less impressed when Mary did a bizarre curtsey and said, "Pleasure to meet you, Julian and Wendi. Do you mind if Horace and I join you? I may have lied. It might be us who are the lonely ones."

"I..." Julian looked to his girlfriend, made a face like he was helpless to say no, like he could not possibly refuse the happy seniors. They looked harmless enough, Horace with his silver hair and Mary, the plump grandmother. "...guess so. Sure. We have some extra chairs in the car."

Wendi gave him a death-stare, mouth pinched tight. Julian merely shrugged, the gutless fool. Politeness had him at the sedan, pulling lawn chairs from the back. He brought them to the fire and gestured for Horace and Mary to sit down. "Make yourselves comfortable," he said.

Horace and Mary sat, then scooched their chairs far enough from the fire so their blood did not feel like acid bubbling beneath their skin.

"Where are you from?" Horace asked.

Julian told him they were from Seattle. "We're driving south to Arizona, camping along the way. This is our first stop."

"Ours too," Horace said. "What are the chances, eh?"

Wendi sighed. Horace and Mary had ruined her envisioned night of romance beneath the stars. She said, "Chances are pretty good. It's a big country, dude. Lots of people go camping."

"They do," Horace agreed. He had gotten a whiff of something delicious. The sweet scent of Wendi's skin, the sweaty tang of her crevice, were wafting up Horace's nose, rousing an animal. "But no one else is camping here tonight. It's just us. Just the four of us for miles."

There was a suggestion in Horace's voice that neither Wendi nor Julian liked. Horace's edge made them nervous. He licked his lips and leaned forward, elbows on his knees, leering at the young couple through the fire with eyes blacker than the void of space. He had forgotten who he was, Horace Steeple. Somewhere in the aroma of skin and charred wood he had lost himself. He had no power to fight the urge and there were terrible things happening in the trees. Shadows of opaque monkeys hung from branches with black, coiled tails and droopy limbs. There were others, ugly beasts crafted of gloom in the shape of giant bats, their wings so large they brushed the forest floor.

Horace said, "Can I ask you something, Julian?"

The boy gulped. "What is it?"

Horace smacked his lips together. When he spoke, his voice came dull and raspy, conjured from a forsaken realm somewhere between man and spirit, where savagery is law and the cruel inhabitants play games of violence and brutality; and God long ago let his light there die, and he relinquished that place and left it to fester, be blighted by sin and corrupted by evil.

"Would you mind if I fuck your girlfriend?"

Julian's eyes bulged from his face as he spat beer all over himself. "Excuse me?"

Horace shifted in his seat, grumbled, "Mm.

Fuck your friend."

Wendi was awash with terror. She clutched Julian's hand and said, "We need to go right now. Julian, get the keys. There's something wrong with these people. Look at their eyes. I think they're on drugs."

Horace and Mary did look crazed. Mary had taken to bouncing in her chair like a demonic imp, her eyes dark and her chanting, "Sex! Sex! Sex!" She wanted it even more than Horace did, and Horace was literally foaming at the mouth, on the edge of his seat as he leered at the young lovers. He had lost control. The lust had killed Horace Steeple. The family man was gone, husband and father eradicated by some godforsaken abomination in control of Horace's body.

"Yeah." Julian eyed the old folk cautiously. "Let's get in the car."

And that was when Mary lost her mind. She yowled and lunged through the fire like an enraged pig and tackled Julian from his chair.

Wendi shrieked and stood up. "What are you doing? Get the fuck off him!"

Horace was on her in a second. He snatched the girl up by her hair and snarled in her face, the feral animal. She cried and scratched and Horace dragged her flailing into her tent, where they were swallowed by the darkness within.

4

Horace stood in the tent's doorway and fastened his belt. He wore no expression but was disheveled and all around his mouth was dark, stained a cannibalistic shade of red. In the tent behind him was a lump, broken and twisted in the dimness, contorted like an acrobat from some disturbed circus, defiled and unmoving.

Mary had Julian in the dirt. She was naked and

gross, riding the boy with her hands pressed against his bare chest and her mouth agape in some hideous expression of ecstasy.

The boy himself lay in turmoil. He stared blankly at the sky. Mary had driven the tent spikes through his cheeks like indigenous piercings. These foreign objects held his mouth open. He looked grotesque, especially with his arms flat beside him and the area where Mary's flabby ass bounced smeared red—from either him or her, no one could say. It was hard to determine whether Mary bounced on Julian's flaccid and bruised member or if he still had one at all. Mary had torn his chest to shreds. She had even bitten off his nipples.

Seeing their sinful endeavor made Horace's hunger return. He dropped his pants and presented himself to Mary, who eagerly sucked his dick while she continued to rape the whimpering boy, there in the stillness of the wood with an audience of shadows peeping from the brush.

Mary finished and got up. Horace was still engorged. He took her place, turned the boy around and forced himself inside. Julian groaned, his mutilated face smooshed in the dirt. He could only cry as Horace fucked him. Horace fucked that boy until his own knees were raw and his cock was chafed. And perhaps he fucked that boy to death.

5

Horace and Mary were clothed and filthy. They lingered near the dead campfire, estranged and without thought. They were more zombies than anything. Horace Steeple was dead in his own body. Whatever occupied it was a foul creation from the deepest pit of gloom.

A shadow then appeared in the doorway of the

couple's tent. It crawled into the night and stood slouched, looking much like Wendi with tousled hair and a thin frame. The shade hung her head in sadness and walked into the forest to join its kin.

The dead kid on the ground twitched and wriggled. His body charred and blackened and dissolved into an onyx goo. The gunk then boiled and bubbled in the dirt and reformed itself into a liquid shadow, which followed its counterpart into the woods and was gone.

Horace and Mary retreated to their own tent in silence. Both were sick in the residue of their indulgences.

Their campsite was dark, the prop fire dead long ago. They retired to their tent and closed the flap and were very robotic. They climbed into large sleeping bags the wrong way, like serpents slithering into their lairs, feet jutting out the openings. They remained like that, shielded from the day and fast asleep in their cocoons, until Helios steered the sun below the Earth and night returned.

They packed up their tent and moved on.

KATELYN & GRANT

1

Katelyn Griffin was ravenous. She could not reconcile her hunger, no matter how much her and Grant devoured. They drove on through the unlit county roads of Utah like stoners with the munchies, chomping on chocolate bars, guzzling energy drinks, eating chips and gas station sandwiches. It was never enough, and Katelyn was sick. She puked out the window and said to Grant, "How did I meet you, anyway?"

Grant shrugged. He was gnawing on the steering wheel as he drove. "I can't remember anything before we set off from Grande Junction. What day is it, Thursday? I'm so hungry. It's hard to think. I know we spent the night—er... the day in Grande Junction. We were at my family reunion, right? I met you at my dad's place?"

Katelyn could not remember. She knew she had left Denver on Tuesday in her own car. She had gone for a hike. It was all a blur after that. She had no idea what happened to Wednesday.

"I need more." Katelyn tossed her empty grocery bag into the back seat. She had eaten thirteen chocolate bars and five greasy gas station sandwiches. Grant was right. It was impossible to think with the hunger turning her inside-out. Katelyn just wanted food. She wanted meat. Fresh meat.

"I'm going to see my mother," she said. "Mamma's dying. She lives in Sacramento. Is that where we're going?"

"I don't think so." Grant was biting his knuckles. "You screamed at the lights of the last city we almost entered. Remember? You said it hurt your blood. Fuckin' hurt mine too. We're on the backroads, somewhere near Salina."

"Utah?"

"Mhm."

There was a ranch up ahead, its lights shining through the starkness. "We should go in there," Katelyn said. "Maybe they have food. We can take it."

"Good idea."

They turned onto the dusty trail and headed for the ranch. In the backseat was a trio of mad shadows without shape or solidity, a crew of ghosts reeling in excitement and pointing with their sooty fingers at the ranch, the old farmhouse alone and bright in the void of grassland.

Grant parked in the driveway and they got out. "We should say we're lost," Katelyn said. "Lost and hungry."

"Got it."

There was an old crone watching them from the window, the curtains parted and her pale complexion like an ugly witch leering at them.

Katelyn said, "Fucking hillbilly."

2

Grant knocked. The lady opened the door just a crack and peeked her mousy face at them.

"What do you want?

"Sorry to bother you," Katelyn said. "We're lost. We tried to take a shortcut to Selina but got lost in this darn maze of backroads. We were hoping you could give us directions."

Katelyn's nose twitched. She could smell the woman's cooking and her tummy growled. "And I have to pee. I hoped I could use your washroom."

The old woman's eyes darted between Katelyn and Grant, suspicious but curious. She did not get many visitors on her lonely ranch. "May as well come in," she said, and swung the door open. "No use standing out in the dark."

Inside the foyer were all the knick-knacks of an old farmstead. Ancient saw blades were balanced on shelves because they were appropriate decoration in that place, and there was a series of strange porcelain dolls situated on the padded seat of a green recliner, an abundance of other oddities displayed throughout.

"Lucky it's me you found," the lady said. She had long silver hair and eyes that shone bright green. "Were my husband, Ernie, still alive, he would have more like than not shot you both in your shoes at the doorstep. Well, at least the darker of you."

"I'm not sure whether to be thankful or sorry," Katelyn said, half smiling. All she could smell was the food, a thousand spices tickling her nostrils and sparking twangs in her stomach. She was so damn hungry.

"Oh, no bother. Ernie's been dead a while. It's just me here now, and I don't mind an intrusion, colored or otherwise. Bathroom's this way. Come on through."

As they walked down the hall, the lady said, "Name's Charlene. I've lived on this ranch all my life, near seventy years now. Don't get much company since Ernie passed. Mostly men from the bank." She gestured to a door at the end of the hall. "Toilet's in there."

Katelyn went into the toilet, sat on the seat while her legs jittered and she chewed on her lip. She just wanted the woman's food. Katelyn did not know why she was so hungry, yet she could not remember a time when she was full. There was so much in her head, really important things screaming her attention—where she was, who Grant was, why she was with him. It was all suffocated by the need to feed. She flushed the toilet and went into the hall.

"Everything in order?" Charlene asked. The lady had a kindness about her that made Katelyn feel guilty about lying.

"Yes. I'm just so hungry. I feel like I'm dying. We best get back on the road. We need to find some food before I fall dead."

"Just so happens I made dinner about an hour ago," Charlene said. She wrung her delicate hands, looking hopeful for some company. "It's still hot if you kids want a plate. I don't mind to share. Haven't got much company since Ernie passed."

"We'd love to," Grant said, no hesitation. His eyes were near as voracious as Kate's were. Together they were starved hyenas, predatory and impatient. They tripped over each other as they chased Charlene through her house, into her kitchen where the smells of marinate pork and fried veggies and fresh bread had Katelyn's eyes rolling in the back of her skull.

3

Katelyn and Grant sat opposite the table while Charlene busied herself at the kitchen counter.

"You kids together?"

"No." Katelyn was salivating as Charlene sliced the ham. "Just friends."

Charlene sighed. "How good of you to say so. That is a relief. You know, if God wanted whites and blacks to breed, he'd not have born us on different shores. Nor with different skin for that matter. No, I reckon we ought to keep our colors to ourselves. Not that I'm saying your people are savages in this country. No, we're all Americans. But still."

Katelyn only half heard the woman's racist rhetoric. It was difficult to hear anything over the thunder of her heart and the grumble of her belly.

Charlene came over with two plates heaped with potatoes, cream corn, carrots, slices of marinated ham, and Katelyn had to dig her nails into her forearm to keep herself from snatching the plates from the old woman and burying her face in them like a dog.

The woman served Grant first, then Katelyn, then sat at the head of the table. "Should we pray?" It was hardly a question.

Difficult for the maniacs to shut their eyes. They wanted to gorge themselves. Charlene reached across the table and placed a hand over Katelyn's and over Grant's. "Dear lord, I want to thank you for the meal we are about to receive..."

Katelyn felt the blood coursing through Charlene's palm, the warmth of it against her skin. She could no longer fight the need, the hunger, the tadpoles swimming in her eyes. Katelyn picked up her fork and stabbed it through the top of Charlene's wrinkly hand.

Charlene screamed, "What are you doing?" and tried to pull away, but Katelyn was stabbing her in the forearm psychotically with a steak knife. Blood squirting over the table, over the food, onto Katelyn's face. She would not let the woman go. Katelyn sunk her teeth into Charlene's arm, sucking the blood that gushed from the knife wounds.

Grant tackled Charlene out of her seat and him and Katelyn growled and fought over the old woman's bloody arm as Charlene screamed and begged for mercy. Her frail heart gave out and she spasmed, going into cardiac arrest as the vultures picked her apart.

4

Katelyn and Grant carved meat from her limbs and ate it despite the rawness and bad taste, then cracked open the brittle bones of her fingers and swallowed the marrow like pixie sticks. It soon became a butcher's kitchen, cannibals given tool and modern device. Katelyn flayed the flesh off Charlene's back with a perry knife while Grant used a serrated blade to hack apart her thigh and cut out small chunks. Then they used the sheets of Mary's peeled skin like tortilla shells and filled them with diced meat, rolled them into tight cigars (the favorite meal of a Mexican headhunter) and ate them raw.

The heathens were naked in their cookery and smeared with blood. They sipped a filthy brine from ceramic bowls, mouths awash in sticky pulp of human.

Carnivores

Katelyn took Charlene's cooked head from the oven and Grant cracked her skull open like a coconut and they used spoons to eat Charlene's brains. Her face was melted, burned, her tongue blackened and stretched over her teeth. They pulled out her eyeballs and ate them, slurped the tendons like noodles.

Katelyn and Grant slept through the day in the pantry in their own pig slop, surrounded by guts and bones like it was an eagle's nest. They woke at dusk and foraged for leftovers and licked blood off the tile floor. Then they showered to be clean and changed into some of Charlene's dead husband's clothes before leaving.

HORACE & MARY

1

Horace was not doing well. He entered the town of Pendleton early Thursday night, around the time Katelyn and Grant were knocking on Charlene's door, with Mary finger-fucking herself in the passenger seat.

Horace was unwell because of the ache in his groin. It kept getting worse. He was unwell because the dead stench of those poor campers was still on his fingers and whatever remnant of Horace Steeple still lived in the corrupted chambers of his mind hated it. Horace Steeple was a thin shred, a lingering speck of humanity, an afterimage of a soul in the black eyes of whatever beast drove into Pendleton

It was the fleeting human who braved the searing lights of the city in search of pleasure, ill-gotten satisfaction from one as degraded as himself.

Mary cackled. "I need it now, darling." And blasted her cunt, folded over herself.

Horace needed it too. His guts convulsed as he drove through middle class neighborhoods, modern houses and reasonably priced cars parked in double-wide driveways. He snarled at the strip mall, still busy with folk sitting inside late-night cafes and twenty-four-hour diners, sushi shops and the rest closed for the night. East of the mini-mall was a concrete overpass where people slept curled inside the thick shadow of its bulk.

Horace and Mary arrived in a dingy area of cracked, lightless apartment buildings riddled with ugly graffiti. The occupants of these decrepit structures peered out of shattered windows at the slow-moving vehicle like the hidden victims of some lingering war. Their peasant brethren meandered through the crummy streets and some pushed shopping carts full of crap. They were dressed in lairs of rag upon rag like traveling merchants from eons past with their wares of discarded junk piled high in their carts. Tarps had been tied to these modern wagons. They flapped in the wind like the flags of crestfallen knights.

The mood darkened inside the truck. Horace breathed harshly and leered out the window. He had found a streetwalker. She was just what he needed to fill the endless void inside him before he moved back onto the desolate byways of America and followed the pull in his mind.

The hooker was ghoulish and decayed in the truck's high beams. She paced the sidewalk, staggering left to right and glancing over her shoulder at irregular intervals with a look of paranoia, her eyes yellow as a coon's and her hair the same.

The truck slowed to a crawl behind the addict. She heard the rumble of its engine and stopped moving, waited on the sidewalk for it to approach.

Then she staggered to the window and knocked on it with a small fist of bone and taut skin.

Horace rolled the window down. "Good evening."

"Whatch'a looking for?" Her voice scratchy, fumigated.

"Company."

"Yer wife too?"

Mary wriggled in her seat, the fat little bitch. "Wife too. Wife Too!"

The creature born from the boiled filth found under bridges and in alleys, dank basement lairs, climbed into the back of the truck and they drove away from the curb in grim silence. The fiend scratched at the back of her hand with craggy nails and her eyes darted nervously.

The streetwalker never did ask their destination, even though they drifted quickly away from the city and its abhorrent lights. She saw an old, kinky couple with a lot of money in need of a toy. The hooker ignored the dread in her rotten guts.

2

The place was far and her captors silent and so still she reckoned they were aliens, and her heart fluttered. She clawed at her ripped jeans, blinked, scratched some more. They turned onto a dirt road and continued while the junkie gripped her seat and stared out the window at darkness. She had not seen the stars in a long time.

They parked in a gravel clearing in the middle of nowhere.

"Get out," Horace said. He had taken a backseat in himself, Horace Steeple so damn hungry for sex he could not stop the infernal influence of the essence within him.

They stood beside the vehicle, the hired flesh

against the door and Mary tittering, Horace's arms folded over his chest as he admired the skittish animal. "Clothes off and hands on the hood."

"It's two hundred for sex," she said. "Four hundred for some fuckin' kinky shit."

Horace said nothing, and his silence frightened the woman but she did as she was told. She stripped naked and put her hands on the hood, shivering with her jeans caught around one ankle and laying in the dirt like a used snake skin. Her flab hung over the sides of her hips, wrinkled like her stomach, like her breasts that sagged, nipples long and rubbery. She breathed in short gasps, so cold.

Horace nudged her feet apart and she spread her legs wide and Horace pushed her face against the chilly metal of the truck's hood. Her flogged her from behind. In the darkness of the bushes at the edge of the sacrificial clearing, the prostitute saw with her yellow eyes something rustle. Small cretins that could have been dogs or anything at all.

Horace steeple bashed her skull open on the hood as he ejaculated inside her. Mary lay in the dirt with her fist in her cunt. They left the whore naked and mangled on the edge of some dusty, nameless road. Horace watched in the rear-view mirror as her blackened spirit left her body and faded into the night, another soul for the shadow king.

Horace and Mary drove on through the haunted lands until the sun tempted to ignite the sky, then they slept to avoid the wrath of daylight, a thing shunned and not seen for days, no longer welcome.

KATELYN & GRANT

Carnivores

1

The road came to a cadaverous conclusion Friday night; a sick finale of gore and crime that would make national news, draw sympathy from those who watched the shocking report on their television sets and cause even the most perverse of men to reel in disgust—the black chambers of their hearts to weep for the desecrated, the madness of it all.

2

Inside a dirty motel on the edge of Twin Falls, Idaho, a dark woman and her companion sat on the edge of their bed and stared blankly at their vague reflections in the glass of an old television screen.
A reckoning rose in the temples of their wasted minds.

These two had no luggage. They had no need for towels or the miniature bottles of soap in the shower. No need for the blanket wrapped tightly over their mattress. They had no desire to bathe, to sleep, to be human. It was as they sat in the hollow room, in the dark, that a manifest was decreed to them by smoke and drifts of spirit that swirled about the room, and that they could see swimming and looming in the reflective glass of the television. The horrible apparitions spoke to them in whispers. They said things only the two soulless ones could hear and understand. And there, with help from the shadows, Katelyn Griffin and Grant Gerald broke their tenuous connection with themselves, becoming dull, and their humanity was forfeit.

They cried black tears and clutched the bedsheet while moaning in agony. They fell to the floor—tumbled off the bed in each other's arms and crashed onto the carpet, quivered and wept and cringed as the remaining purity of their souls was tainted, a pain greater than fire or fist or humiliation

101

breaking them from the inside.

They rose together after a time and left the room. Kate and Grant stood on the second-floor balcony of the motel and looked down into a pool of filth and soggy leaves. Somewhere a woman cried out in pleasure. Somewhere a man yelled. They turned right and walked to their neighbor's door and knocked.

3

There was the sound of frantic movement and then the door opened and a man's scraggly face peeked between the thin crevice afforded by the lock-chain. The stink of cigarette smoke seeped outwards and a TV blared within.

"This about the noise?" The man was out of breath, his eyes red and suspicious.

"No," Grant said.

The skinny man glanced between Katelyn and Grant, whose faces were stained charcoal as if they had applied too much mascara and it washed down their cheeks in the rain. "Then what the fuck do you want?"

Grant sniffed. He peeked over the man's head and saw a heap of paraphernalia scattered on the ground in a style most ritualistic; tinfoil, two lighters, a shattered light bulb, vials, a metal cylinder, all glittering like treasures in the flicker of the television.

"We have money," Grant said. "We're fuckin' hungry, man. We can pay. I tell you now we got enough."

The junkie eyed them suspiciously, then unbolted the door and let them in.

Katelyn and Grant entered and shut the door behind them. The place stank. Dirty clothes littered the floor. The pale, emaciated man in his white tank top and loose jeans strolled to his nest and crouched, pushed around some baggies with his fingers. "I don't got much."

"We don't need much," Katelyn said.

A mutilation soon laid in the lame glow of the tv. The scoundrel's forearms had been dug open to create red trenches and the bone in those gullies was white. His face was unharmed. It stared falsely up at Katelyn and Grant as they ate. He tasted like bleach.

4

A woman opened the next door that Katelyn and Grant knocked on and gasped at the abysmal sight of them. "My god, are you alright?"

The woman was middle aged, small and her eyes pathetic and somehow orange in the dusk of the room. She was frail. Grant pushed the woman backwards into her temporary habitat and hit her head and she fell unconscious to the floor.

She was thin and tasted of old yogurt. It was disgusting. They first gnawed on her face because the way it was dormant and in peace made them angry. She awoke during the first few bites and screamed, and Grant stood and separated her jaw from her head with his foot.

They used leverage to snap her bones, their teeth to rip away skin and cut the tendons that held her limbs together. When done, the small woman was broken in a bundle of human sticks and they used those pieces as chew toys, nibbled off the skin until they were bloated and sick and they sat panting in a den of tattered cloth and bones strewn about.

There was another door and another lonely victim, an old man on his way to visit his grandchildren. They consumed him and moved on to the next.

Katelyn and Grant were untethered, fit to burst. Their stomachs pulsed. Their throats were raw and half their teeth were either chipped or broken into jagged fangs. As they knocked on the fourth door they truly looked like necromorphic fiends, things risen from the grave by dark magic and sent to terrorize the living.

A lone traveler answered the door, and like the others, dropped his jaw in surprise at how gory the intruders were. The mad zombies pushed into the room and both Katelyn and Grant vomited pieces of old man onto the traveler's duffel bag and he watched in horror as bits of human were spat from them and they shit their pants and pissed themselves. Then they staggered like drunks after the traveler as he dashed for a corner of the room and tried to dial 911 on his phone.

He hit 9, then 1, then was beaten against the wall until he slumped onto his ass. Surely someone should have heard the man scream. The hungry defilers clawed at his guts with sharp nails, frantic as rodents and snarling all the while until their greedy fingers broke through his outer shell and his guts spilled out and Katelyn and Grant jammed their heads into the tear in the man's stomach.

They knocked on more doors.

More until none.

5

They dripped and their shoes made wet, sloshing sounds as they walked across the parking lot to Grant's truck. None of their skin was visible under the coating of black crimson they were drenched in. Slop rolled from their chins and down their shirts. They left a trail of it in their wake.

In the morning, there were police by the dozen and every room in that hotel was inspected and dusted and the officers on site regurgitated on the concrete and called their families and told them that they loved them. The owner of the hotel sat with his back against a wall and he stared stupefied at the parking lot, the blare of blue and red lights.

An A.P.B was broadcast nation wide, the names of Katelyn Griffin and Grant Gerald. By noon of Saturday, a man-hunt had been called to order and hundreds of police picked through the city and established road blocks and combed the countryside.

They would not find them. Katelyn and Grant were parked near Glenn's Ferry all day Saturday, so far from any road and so caked in dirt and dust that no one could have see them where they slept, there in the cab, curled together and bestrewn in one another's nausea. Only the sun bore witness to their diseased hibernation, its all-seeing eye a flare of angry justice that burned them with rays that broke through the tinted windows and scorched their flesh.

HORACE & MARY

1

Mack's Creek Park, near the city of Nampa. A dimly lit campground on the edge of a riverbend so large it looked like a lake, the water gentle in its motion and the hills beyond a dreamy backdrop. Docks extended into the water and little boats rocked peacefully beside them. There were three motorhomes parked there, three families sitting around their campfires and the air festive for the weekend.

Horace and Mary were already soulless when they entered the park, towing behind them a shroud of darkness so thick the stars blotted at their arrival and the peaceful hills darkened into mounds of coal. Trees shuddered and bristled and things slithered onto branches and leered at the jolly campers from their twisted nests.

Those campers were subject to the impending doom. The jovial mood shared by the park's occupants soured as the depraved ones approached, and their fires flared an angry shade of red.

Horace parked the Chevy sideways at the entrance; a crude barricade. He and Mary walked from there, down the gravel path, past the silent ranger's cabin, and into the grove of the left-most campsite.

2

A mother wrinkled her nose and narrowed her eyes in the sudden eclipse of gloom. Something was wrong. She crossed her legs, pale thighs and flower shorts, and shivered. Her husband sat upright in his lawn chair and pocketed his cold beer. He threw a concerned glance toward the trees, ominous limbs swaying in a sudden breeze. Their children, young and happy. They roasted wieners over the campfire with care-free ardor. Them, the kids, fisherman hats and black fingers and scrapes on their filthy knees. They were bright in such a bleak eventide, and their innocence radiated brilliantly against the cruel darkness. Though for all their purity nothing could break through the suppressive melancholy suffocating the park and everyone in it.

Because they were part of the plan, the scheme, the motion of events uncontrollable and bound to repeat; slain, eaten, burned, desecrated, agitated to life in a cauldron of insanity, bloodlust, mad desire, an insatiable evil that laminated itself over the world and refused to leave. It had no purpose but to maim and maul, to abduct and violate and add to its army of shadow. It was belched from below and on the

Earth it stayed.

The smiling youngsters looked up and saw a reaper in a knit shirt with eyes black as the coal in their fire. They did not comprehend. They gazed curiously from below the brims of their floppy hats at Horace, who approached through the trees with a rifle in both hands like a mad hunter.

A bullet impacted one of the boy's skulls and exited the back and he fell sideways into the flames, which began to char his skin and kindle his blonde hair like dry straw. The brother of that boy looked stupidly at Horace as he reloaded the rifle and pulled the trigger. A bullet tore through the boy's chest and into his tiny, beating heart and he rolled dead in the dirt.

Horace strode forward and cocked the rifle and shot the mother dead as she rose from her chair. The father also stood, tried to yell, but instead grunted and fell to the ground with a hole in his neck and blood sputtering out.

Horace fled, an assassin in the night.

Mary, the little hobgoblin, a devil's grin and malice on her face, descended through the brush and onto the corpses, chortling to herself like a pig.

3

Horace walked down the park's only road with his rifle in hand, a mad-dog soldier turned on his own kind, bent on the slaughter of all humanity due to a fracture in his mind that could not be reconciled.

A woman came into view. She heard the shots and ran to investigate. She was murdered and bleeding on the gravel road before she could discern the gun totting lunatic for what he was. Horace came upon her body, stepped over it, and followed her route down a short hill, between some saplings, and to a large white motorhome.

Blinking eyes peeked between the blinds. Horace tried to open the door. It was locked. He looked at the nervous peepers and raised his rifle and fired.

Glass shattered. Someone screamed. The door burst open and a man in cargo shorts unloaded three shots from a pistol at Horace and every round missed. Horace jabbed the man in the guts with the barrel of his rifle and fired. Ooze exploded from the back of him, all over the trailer walls and his body was rocketed into a closet where it collapsed.

Horace climbed inside and picked up the dead man's revolver. He looked around. It was quiet. He strolled by the fold-up tables littered with magazines and chip bags, family night in a family's motorhome. He came to a bathroom door and kicked it with the toe of his boot. Locked. He pointed the revolver at the door and fired the remaining three rounds. He then bashed the door's lock with the heavy wooden butt of his rifle until the flimsy thing cracked and the door swung inwards.

A teenage girl sat on the toilet. Her head hung and she drooled blood onto the floor, a wet darkness spreading over her pink tank top. She looked at Horace and pleaded with her eyes, opened her mouth to speak but her life spilled out between her lips and onto her white shorts. She fell forward with the same ugly grace those who die on the toilet all share.

Somewhere outside an engine groaned, chugged, and came alive. Horace hastened to the shattered window and looked out to see headlights break through the density of trees and he heard the squeal of spinning tires and the spray of gravel.

He ran outside to the road, just in time to witness a truck speed towards the exit in a huff of exhaust, try and crash through Marcus' ol' Chevy and instead come to a dramatic halt and a horn blared.

He approached the wrecked truck, smoke seeping from its bent hood. There was a woman and her children inside, some injured and all in shock. He executed them through the glass; one shot, two, three, four, the youngsters deceased in their seats and the mother's head slumped against the airbag as if it were a pillow.

Horace pulled them from the wreckage and into the night. He hauled the mother and her offspring to an empty lot at the edge of the river, then went back for the rest.

4

Horace Steeple dragged the victims of his motorhome massacre by their legs to the river, then the slain family, their son, his face melted beyond recognition.

The cadavers were piled together and Mary stripped them of their clothes, kiddy as a gremlin and fat and ugly in the pitch, the way she swayed and hunched over the bodies on the bank of the river like a water dwelling monster crawled to the shore in search of carrion.

There were eleven warm bodies displayed naked at the water's edge. Each was fresh and sticky, varying in shape and size and vulgarity of wound. Some still wept blood.

Although they were emptied of life, they were soft enough to penetrate and malleable enough to masquerade as passionate lovers in a rotten orgy, an immoral parade of sex and self indulgence, there on the dark shore where necrophiliacs were born and turned loose on the mound of dead, frenzied and wicked, insatiable rapists ravaging one stark victim after the next, dancing with them in a lewd tango, a performance of sexual deviation by those practitioners of the deepest perversion.

OTAKTAY'S SALVATION

IN LIFE,
VIOLENCE.

IN DEATH,
VIOLENCE

1

Daybreak at Bruneau Canyon.

Otaktay stood on the edge of a bowl carved in the canyon wall, peering into the depths of the gap as yellow light filled it and turned the shale a brilliant hue of gold. The crater looked like the indentation of a meteor strike, and Otaktay stepped carefully into it, lowered himself onto his haunches and slid down, one hand guiding him through the loose rubble and the other on his axe.

He came to a stop at its edge and looked behind him, up that slanted semi-circle. There was no way back. Otaktay treaded carefully along the fringe of the crater to a rocky bulge, gave it a fierce hug and shimmied down to in-between two vertical columns like a filthy Santa.

The chute ended in a tight nook and he stood dizzy looking up. The spines of rock extended far above his head, and above them only sky. He was in a pocket on the canyon wall. He stepped onto another ramp of loose shale, lowered his body in the position of a crab and slowly skidded down the gravelly incline. He had thought it not too steep, but it was. He lost control, fell and drifted off the edge of a precipice and fell like a stone fifteen feet to the ground below.

2

Many miles south of Mountain Home, away from the busy lanes of the interstate, beyond the twisted Snake River, laid the small hamlet of Bruneau. It was a sleepy town in Owyhee County, positioned on the edge of the prairies, the land of desert plains and deep canyons.

Carnivores

Folk there were restless Saturday night. They lay in bed and fought for sleep, tossed and turned while dark and disturbing images played behind their eyes and unwanted thoughts of violence danced in their heads. Some of these people rose and stood tormented in the dusk of their bedrooms, stared down at their sleeping spouses and wrestled horrible desires. Children cried in their beds. Old women stood on porches and stared up at the cracks of black lightning that skirted the sky, the swell of opaque clouds that consumed each other; the great moon that dominated above, blood red and scowling.

A black Silverado entered Bruneau and thunder rolled across the flat lands. Civilians cowered in their homes, under blankets, shivering and afraid. The truck continued east, away from the town until another blocked its path, this other machine idling between lanes with its headlights off.

The Silverado turned off its lights too. The ghost trucks idled bumper to bumper for several minutes then proceeded side by side down the secluded highway 78, and turned onto the even more lonesome 51.

3

South along a vacant stretch of nothing that led to nowhere, so they roamed, a coalition of rumbling hearses. Further still through the waste, the open country, the domain of shrub and tumbleweed. At first, a few darkened homes and plots of land, but soon the territory became void of life and the road's existence was a wonder itself. Why build such a pointless length of asphalt, a redundant artery across state lines, if it were not a passage where evil flowed north to south, south to north—the comings and goings of masked men and nefarious females obscured by night's desolate cowl?

They turned right, onto an unmarked and unpaved road. The people inside the trucks jostled and grumbled insanely when they ran down small animals. They were not human, these people. Not anymore. They were husks of the damned, summoned to a place of great evil by a thing more wretched than themselves.

A sign read: *Now Entering the Shoshone-Paiute Tribe Wildlife Reserve*

The region had been given that name in respect of the first nation to have lived on and prospered from the land, not two centuries before. Though now it was a wasted, unvisited land.

The path reached its end. The trucks stopped. Dust swirled behind them in a misty nebula. The people got out. They walked a few feet and stood side by side in the darkness of a sun-scorched world, a quartet of grizzly, disheveled strangers all languid and stained and repugnant in their ugliness and each gazing ahead at a pale cabin, which seemed as old as the dirt itself, a haunted remnant of a sand covered age.

From the gloom of the interior came a man in a wide brim hat and a long coat, his face obscured by shadow. He leaned in the doorframe and smoked, a frontier man baked in the red of the old west. Behind the cabin loomed a crimson moon, these lost relics caught in its angry maw and it rested on the crust of the Earth.

4

Otaktay opened his eyes to a crepuscular world of jagged outlines and barbed vision. His head was in agony and his jaw felt swollen to twice its size. He lay dumb beneath a fir tree, staring up through its pointy limbs.

Otaktay groaned and rolled onto his belly. He

could hear the river flowing somewhere near him and he crawled towards the noise through moist grass and soil, to a shore of pebbles. He dunked his head into the churning black water and drank for the first time in days.

It was 9:47 PM on Friday, four days since Onida's death.

He chugged water until his stomach bloated, then pulled his head from the river and gasped, laid back and panted. Night had crept up on him while he slept. He was without a sanctuary of light, alone on the bottom of Bruneau Canyon.

He sprang to his feet and looked around. The valley floor held no ominous shadows other than those the moon cast behind the short trees and whatever strangeness stirred in the murk of the floor. He knew the haunts would be upon him soon. He wondered why they were not already. He also knew there was no time to build five fires. Otaktay thought to use his flint to set the entire floor ablaze to ward off the shadows.

Only one problem. He was naked.

Otaktay groped for his satchel and realized his loin cloth and his tiny bag of tricks were gone, lost somewhere amongst the debris of the slope or in the branches of the tree he had fallen through. He knew right then he was doomed. Thinking fast, Otaktay foraged for two large stones on the bank of the river and clanked them together in a sad attempt to make sparks, but of course nothing happened. The brush down there was too moist to ignite.

That was when they came.

They could have taken him at nightfall—laid claim to his body as it sprawled limp in the grass. Yet they had bided their time. They had lingered unseen in a world between the living and the dead and waited for Otaktay to awake. The shadows were a sadistic lot.

They wished Otaktay to suffer profoundly in his final moments of humanity, and to gaze upon their featureless faces at his time of surrender.

He caught sight of the first malformed shade beneath the tree he had woke under. It was black and short and oddly shaped, a gloomy garden gnome leering at him from under the canopy, in which even more sinister forms lurked. The whole tree was alive with limbs that writhed like anacondas from branch to branch and Otaktay was sure he could see inside the dark grove of pine needles to where bodies were entwined in a sick orgy of darkness.

He turned downriver. The sloshing water went straight for a distance then veered left and was gone. There was a brief shore of pebbles and a plain of short grass and upon that meadow was a lone shadow in the shape of a scarecrow, adorned with a wide brim hat. He stood vigilant and still, a lifeless sentinel in a farmer's field, and Otaktay voiced his defiance to this solitary mirage.

"You won't take me. Not like her. Not like Onida."

The sound of his resistance echoed through the valley of shadows and none returned his cry. He pivoted to face the nest of black serpents held within the tree and announced his purpose.

"I am the hunter. Me! I am the ancient blood of this place and it is you who should fear me. I knew there was a reason for my training, for all my years of torment. It was to fight you. That's why they chose me. The elders knew one day I would face the darkness, and that I would send it back to Hell!"

Sadly, Otaktay sent nothing anywhere. The air thickened into a smog, became tangible, and a shadow flourished before him. It pressed its hand against the

Indian's chest. The touch was gentle, almost cordial. The shadow bent into the likeness of a man and pushed Otaktay into the river.

He hit the water and sank, was pulled beneath the swell and carried turbulent on the undertow. Inside that murky brook were the figures of drowned men and women, stretched into howling ghosts and mangled by the current. The water they sailed through was inky, spoiled by a squid's refuse. Tendrils of gunk curled around Otaktay and penetrated his every orifice. His last thought as the black solution filled him was that he had died, and that he jostled violently through the river of the underworld alongside the souls of the damned.

5

Otaktay stood dripping on the shore as dawn's pink light flooded the canyon. He was forced to walk through the brightness to the place where he had entered the valley. He found his axe laying in a tuft of grass beneath the tree. He reclaimed it and went to work hacking low branches off that same tree. While he labored, the sun beat down on his tawny flesh and its toxic rays made his skin itch, his ears ring, his head quake, and his eyes wish to bleed. It was nauseating, and the moment he gathered enough branches, Otaktay staggered through the morning glare to a small grotto in the wall.

He climbed inside and used the tree limbs to construct a shabby barrier that shielded him from the blight of day. He sat naked in the cavern and cross-legged and did not sleep.

6

When twilight prevailed against the forces of light, Otaktay kicked apart the barricade of wood and abandoned his shelter.

Saturday night he found easy passage out of the

canyon by scaling the western wall. It took no more than an hour and he was soon meandering west again over the great basin of Southern Idaho.

He was not alone. Otaktay trudged across the sunless realm of dirt and rock, a gloomy dreamscape, some perpetually darkened purgatory, with a score of shadows guiding him every mile.

In his mind was singular intent. He sought violence long overdue and the hordes of shadow cheered him onwards to that savage end. On and on they celebrated his naked march. On and on he advanced with his axe brandished and he was invigorated and fueled by the cries that rang from the shady congregation, so enthralled that he burst into a frantic run and sprinted across the dusty plain, his hair fluttering behind him.

It was the witching hour as Otaktay raced headlong through the deadlands, and all the unseen menaces of the world were returning to their lairs. Ghouls in their forest dwellings picked skin from teeth with toothpicks of human bone. The wrathful buried their victims and the macabre predators froze their meat. Incinerators roared, reduced faces to ash and organs to amber. All the sick and all the hungry and all the violent villains concluded their monstrous rituals and prepared for another day of normality; and finally, Otaktay came upon an old, pale, decrepit cabin amid a barren land.

7

An orgy of disturbing noises seeped from the building's cracked walls and rippled across the waste. Otaktay followed them. He approached the haunted cabin, the specter of an estranged hermit's shack found somewhere in the deep woods, uprooted and displaced in time and dumped in the desert—and walked to the front porch.

The door was open. Animalistic sounds drifted down the steps; muffled gasps and grunts of two or more people in the depths of sexual bliss.

Otaktay climbed the steps sneering. He was angry, nostrils flared as he thumped his feet on the old wooden planks. The sound of indulgence enraged him, infuriated the blight in his blood. How dare they bring their deviance to his land, to his native home. Otaktay gripped his axe tight as he came upon the threshold.

Beyond was a dusky room. The interior was burnt. The fireplace was scorched black and the bricks of the chimney smoke-stained. The floorboards were charred. Walls dingy, faded, marked by flame. In the center of the otherwise bare room were people.

They writhed and thrust and were vague in the gloom, the source of the sick din, an audio like a pack of feasting hyenas. Otaktay stepped inside and saw just how gruesome the scene was, bestiality and lust gone wrong; starved canines forced into a habitat of horny apes, each the tormentor and each the tormented. A room of ravenous carnivores.

Horace's face was strained as he slammed into Katelyn's bare ass, black eyes raised to the ceiling and both hands on Katelyn's hips. Katelyn was bent over like a dog, her face buried in Mary's crotch, the old woman laying with her legs arched as if in childbirth, resting on her elbows and watching the black girl chew on her lower lips, pull the skin with her teeth so it stretched and snapped and bled. Katelyn swallowed a piece, then sunk her pincers back into Mary's vagina.

It was a threesome unlike anything ever enacted, even in the perverted corners of snuff and underground kink, chains and whips and abuse.

Grant watched the fuck fest from the corner,

where he was slumped against the wall crying tears of oil and gnawing on his wrist. He had bitten into his forearm and worked it like a stick of corn. Six inches of bone showed and there was nothing between his hand and elbow except skeleton. He was currently trying to flay the skin off his wrist and palm with his broken teeth.

No one noticed Otaktay trembling with rage in the doorway. Horace plowed into Katelyn and Katelyn continued to eat the sensitive parts of Mary, her head between the woman's cellulite-ridden thighs.

The Indian rioted. He threw up his axe and unleashed a murderous cry, rushed forward and swung the dull side of his axe down on Mary's cranium with both hands.

Her head split at the top and Mary crumpled to the floor. Her legs were still arched, Katelyn still eating. Otaktay bawled and brought the heel of his foot down on Mary's eye socket until her face was mush and Katelyn snarled and licked at the gape of a wound where Mary's hairy vagina had been.

Horace was next. Otaktay ran at the sweaty old criminal and reeled his axe upwards into his stomach.

Horace stammered, tried to keep humping. Otaktay plunged his axe into Horace's gut again, dragging the blade sideways and opening a pocket in Horace, his skin peeling open like a zipper. His innards spilled over Katelyn's backside. She lost interest in the dead woman's mutilated genitals and began to lap up the slop laying in a pile on the floor near Horace's dead body.

Otaktay screamed and severed Katelyn's head with one swing of his axe while she had her face buried in a coil of intestines. It rolled, floated through the pool of blood and came to a stop with her virgin eyes staring lifeless at the naked Indian. She still looked hungry.

Otaktay huffed and puffed, soaked in carnage and beyond mad. He marched through the lagoon of slaughter, to Grant, who was now working on the bits of flesh left on his fingers.

Otaktay's axe snapped Grant's chewed wrist at the bare bone like a brittle twig and it fell to the ground. Grant looked at it, confused, then chomped down on his other hand.

"No!"

Otaktay threw his axe across the room and descended on Grant. He sat in the man's lap and slapped his face. He pulled Grant's nipples and gouged his eyes and flailed, wild, insensible. Otaktay spat and yelled and punched and shoved his hand down Grant's throat to the elbow. Grant choked. He was trying to bite, but his jaws would not close. Otaktay plunged his arm all the way into Grant's chest cavity and Grant suffocated and died.

8

Grant's body was thrown with the rest, where Otaktay, in a mad finale, reigned down upon the bodies with his axe. An arm flew, a head was crushed, a leg bone was split in the middle. Otaktay was lost in a frenzy, bits and pieces of Katelyn Griffin, Horace Steeple, Mary Shepherd, and Grant Gerald flung about the derelict cabin like a gore room in a haunted house on Halloween.

Otaktay calmed. The black slime inside his eyeballs dimmed slightly. Were he not naked and covered in anatomy he might have looked human.

He lay on the slippery floor and smiled with satisfaction at a job well done, a duty fulfilled, and at the long night to come. The monsters were mush on the floorboards and the shadows filtered through their blood like leeches. Otaktay's anger had triumphed, the anger of the thing that had claimed his sister and spurned him across the desert. With all the strength he could muster, Otaktay, brother of Onida, reversed his axe into his own face.

Yet did not die.

He groaned and went blind, his nose torn off and his teeth shattered, sprinkled onto his tongue. He had to smack himself twice more before one eye popped from its socket and his brain hemorrhaged.

9

A weathered man entered the building. He wore a wide brim hat and a heavy duster, his black boots thumping over the floorboards as he circled Otaktay's carnage. The sight of it made him smile, the blood and dismemberment. He tipped his hat to the fireplace and the hearth erupted in flames.

The butcher's shop floor of mangled parts and rags bloomed in a fidgety incandescence thrown from the fireplace. The man approached it, kicking aside the limbs of the desecrated with his boots, and reached into the roaring hearth.

His sleeves caught flame. He stepped back, held out his arms and let the fire consume his jacket. He never stopped smiling, big white teeth gleaming from his woolly beard.

The man was a pillar of flame, his hat yellow and pointed like the tip of a candle. He strolled to the epicenter of Otaktay's mad destruction and sat down, cross-legged, amidst the remains of his design.

The cabin was a box of fire. Smoke escaped from the windows in clouds and surged out of the short chimney. The exterior, somehow, remained unburnt.

Watching from the night plains outside was a

legion of countless shadows. They saw through the doorway a ballroom of dancing djinn, all yellow and red and orange and twirling around their burning master where he sat.

Eventually, the inferno ceased to rage. The interior went dark and only a faint heat lingered. The man in the wide brim hat stood, brushed the ashes from his coat, and stepped outside. He no longer smiled. An expression of discontent had his sun-beaten face wrinkled. He scowled at the ghosts before him like they were memories he could not escape.

He walked down the stairs and the horde of corrupt souls parted to allow him passage through their ranks, as would an army for their king. Then they were gone and the desert was quiet. The shadows returned to the wretched abyss from which they came and always will come. The man went back to brood on his flaming stone until next he might unleash his scorn.

J. Cortex

The End

www.ingramcontent.com/pod-product-compliance
Lightning Source LLC
Chambersburg PA
CBHW021129070726
47591CB00014B/1902